Two Peas

Nathan Monk

Copyright © 2017 by Nathan Monk

All rights reserved.

Book design by Nathan Monk

No part of this book may be reproduced in any form or by any electronic or mechanical means including information storage and retrieval systems, without permission in writing from the author. The only exception is by a reviewer, who may quote short excerpts in a review.

This book is a work of fiction. Names, characters, places, and incidents either are products of the author's imagination or are used fictitiously. Any resemblance to actual persons, living or dead, events, or locales is entirely coincidental.

Nathan Monk

Visit my website at
https://www.facebook.com/nathan.monk.90

Printed in PRC

First Printing: November 2017

iSystems Limited
Napier, New Zealand

ISBN: **1540347311**

ISBN-13: 9**78-1540347312**

Two Peas & A Pod

DEDICATION

To Rachel, Isabelle, Declan and Amelia, who all stand beside me through all my crazy endeavours.

ACKNOWLEDGMENTS

I wish to thank the following for all their assistance in proofing and editing. Rachel Monk, Andrew Currie, Sarah Currie, Rachel Mackay, Isabelle Monk, Tracey Wogan

1

May 1, 1997

The labour pains were intense, the pain bearing down on Paula in waves. Each contraction brought pain that tumbled over the prior one, the next starting before the first had even begun to recede. It was as if each new contraction was fighting to be the champion. Paula stared at the ceiling tiles above her and tried to count the holes in each tile before the next contraction arrived. Each time the number got less.

Nurse Samantha Scott mopped Paula's forehead with a wet cloth. She hid her contempt for her patient behind a carefully crafted professional facade. How could this young woman, only just a woman she reminded herself, get herself in this position? Pregnant with triplets?

She was quite a beautiful girl, who Samantha was told, came from a moneyed family. Well, right now Paula looked like hell. Samantha wondered if hell was what they were about to put her through. What they were going to do, what she was a complicit partner in, although illegal, was the right thing to do. Well, that's what she kept telling herself. The $10,000 in her bank account and the better life she could now afford, added another reason to ignore the guilty feelings nagging her conscience. Another scream of pain jarred Samantha out of the second thoughts. It would be soon, she knew. She had already called Dr Kirkland, to explain that the theatre was being readied.

The door to the room opened, and two orderlies came in. "He's ready now Nurse Scott." Samantha turned back to

Paula, "We are taking you to the theatre now Paula, one of your babies is in distress. They will need to be born by Caesarean. Dr Kirkland is all ready for you; I will see you after the surgery. All Paula could do was to nod, the pain was no longer coming in waves, it was now an all-consuming entity. A small bump, as the orderlies started to move the bed, panicked Paula. Looking for a friendly face, she found none.

Nurse Scott remained behind in the room as Paula was wheeled off to the theatre. There was much to do, and much could still go wrong, as she turned to exit the room a nervous looking woman entered. "Mrs Kirkland, how are you..." "Is everything ready?" Olivia Kirkland asked interrupting Samantha. "Yes, Ms Johnson is in quite a lot of pain..." "Not about the girl, is the baby all right?" Mrs Kirkland interrupted again. "Yes I think so, they have just gone to the theatre now." Mrs. Kirkland leant up against the wall and put her head in her hands. "Are we doing the right thing?" she muttered into her hands. Samantha stepped over to her, "Just remember, the girl is very young, and there is no way she can cope with three babies, you are doing her a favour." Mrs Kirkland nodded her head, she was desperate for a child and what Samantha said was true, the girl could not manage three little ones, not without a husband or a supportive family.

Paula began to wake up; the world seemed to be fuzzy then slowly, ever so slowly things started to take form. The room was bright and airy, but unlike the rooms for most new mothers, there were no flowers, no teddy bear soft toys to celebrate the arrival of new life. Those that knew of her pregnancy had long ago cast her out. "One does not have a baby out of wedlock," her mother had said. She had tried to persuade Paula to have them terminated. Paula's mother and father would only call it that, termination, not abortion.

It was like Paula had cancer, a tumour. Her parents had thought it was the solution. All Paula need to do, to fix her life, was consent for 'it' they would never refer to the babies as 'them', to be cut out. Her life, and by extension their lives, could just go on as if this dreadful thing had never happened. Paula's refusal to have an abortion was the last straw, she had been cast out of the family lest she is a reminder of everything her so-called Christian parents stood for. Her friends had been equally unsupportive, words such as 'slut' and 'loose' were uttered behind her back while all the time they advised her to get the babies removed.

2

To Paula, it was one night of wild passion with a guy who did not love her and had no interest in being the dad to three children. She had regretted it from the moment it happened, but that all changed the moment Paula felt the small flutters of life growing in her abdomen. From that point on Paula knew she needed to give birth and, regardless of the challenges, raise these three children.

As the fuzz of the anaesthetic wore off, she suddenly remembered that she had just become the mother of three. Fumbling for the nurse call button, Paula finally managed to press it after the fourth attempt. A buzzer sounded somewhere out in the corridor, and it was not long before she could hear approaching footsteps.

Nurse Scott had been dreading this moment for the last hour. Her patient had slept blissfully unaware of the chess board like movements that Dr Kirkland and his staff had put in play. The final move in the game came now, and it all rested on her shoulders. With this one move, they would win or loose. Taking a big breath she opened the door and went in. Paula was lying on the bed with a drip in her arm providing fluids. Her training kicked in, and she started to check Paula's vitals. The routine of checking pulse, blood pressure, and temperature, made what she was about to say easier.

"My babies, are they all right, where are they?" Paula asked. Samantha looked at Paula with a small measure of compassion and took her hand. "There is some bad news.

You delivered triplets, a boy, and identical twin girls, but I'm sorry the baby boy did not survive." Tears rolled down Paula's face, "But the girls, the twins?" the question seemed to hang in the air as Paula was clinging to the last vestiges of hope. Samantha smiled, "Both are doing well, healthy birth weight, one was five pound two ounces. And the other five pound, and only a little jaundice. They are in the nursery at the moment, just while you had a bit of time to recover. I will go and get them for you now if you like?" "Oh yes please, quickly please." Paula was still sobbing, but it was hard to know if the tears were happy or sad.

Nurse Scott left the room and returned within five minutes pushing a wheeled bassinet. Nestled inside were two perfect little babies. "We thought they would prefer to be together" Samantha explained, "After all, they have been together for their whole lives." She smiled. "Would you like to try to feed them?" Paula nodded, the moment, with all its emotion, was making it hard to find words.

Nurse Scott gently explained the correct hold and how to get the babies to latch on. It would seem that both the twins and Paula were a quick study. As soon as a nipple came within reach each baby hungrily fed. As Paula looked down at her two perfectly formed babies she smiled. "Have you decided on their names?" Samantha asked as she changed the babies diapers. Paula had thought long and hard about this for over five months. "I was going to call my him Daniel Seth, and the twins Gina Violet & Stephanie Rose." "What lovely names, I will fill those out on the birth certificates for you. Shall I take these two back to the nursery now?" "NO!" Paula almost shouted. Nurse Scott looked shocked; this was not the voice of a silly teenager who got knocked up, this was the voice of a protective mother lion. She wondered if she was doing the right thing after all. "I'm so sorry," Paula began to cry again, "I have lost one and can't bear to be apart from these two, I did not mean to be so rude just now." Paula sobbed. "That's ok, I quite understand, but if you need a rest just press the buzzer and I will pop them back to the nursery."

Paula began to say something then stopped. "What is it, Ms Johnson?" Paula looked up with tears in her eyes, "Do you think I could see the baby boy?" Samantha crossed to the side of the bed and took Paula's hand again. "The doctor said to say no if you asked. The baby was born grossly deformed, and he wants to spare you the pain. It is best that you focus on these two now, try not to think about the one that died." Paula wiped the tears with the corner of her sleeve and nodded as she looked down at the two perfectly formed babies. Perhaps it was for the best not to see him, she thought.

Outside the nursery window, the Doctor and Mrs Kirkland looked in. There was only one child in the nursery at this point, a baby boy just born. The label on the bassinet read "James Kirkland". At that moment James started to cry, it was a hungry cry of a baby wanting food. At the same time, the fed and contented twins, Gina and Stephanie Johnson, wrapped in their mother's arms began to cry half a hospital away.

3

Jan 5, 2013

Paula looked at herself in the mirror, not bad, not bad at all. Dennis, her husband, liked to joke that he had won not only the trophy wife but also the trophy twins when he married Paula six years ago. Paula certainly did not look like someone who had delivered twins - triplets, really.

In fact looking at Paula, you would hardly believe she was the mother of teenage girls. Looking in the mirror now she saw a reflection, not just of a trim body and her long blonde hair but a vision of a confident woman who had made a success of her life. She was an average height and of slim build. The weight she had put on carrying the triplets had fallen off but not due to gravity; it had been a hard-won return to her almost pre-pregnancy weight and shape. Her bust had been about the only thing that did not return to how it was. Before feeding the hungry twins she had been a B cup on a good day. After feeding the twins, she had remained a pretty decent C cup.

It would be a lie to say the first few years with Gina and Stephanie had been easy. They were alone and cut off from her family Paula picked and fought many battles, many of which she had won. The achievement she was most proud of, after her amazing twin girls, was completing not only a degree but then Masters in History at Ede University in Denver. Hours spent pouring over textbooks, the girls asleep in their cot, then hours writing assignments as the girls played and babbled away in a language that only twins seemed to understand. Yes, hard work, but looking back now those days held wonderful memories. Moments like the first smiles, rolling over, crawling, Steph getting stuck under furniture, their first steps. The memories still brought a smile to Paula's face.

"You're thinking about the girls." Dennis' voice broke through her thoughts. She hadn't noticed him walk in the room, "How can you always tell?" She asked softly with a smile. Dennis moved to stand behind her. Wrapping his arms around Paula. "Well, two things, first you are always thinking about the girls and second you have this little distant look and a unique half smile."

That comment made her laugh as she turned inside his arms to embrace him face to face. "Always thinking about the girls am I?" As she gave his butt a friendly tease. Dennis pulled her closer, "Do we have time?" He asked with a sly grin on his face. "Pervert, is that all you ever think of, sex? And NO we do not have time." Paula paused. "Perhaps later," She said breaking out of his embrace to finish getting ready.

Dennis followed her to the walk in wardrobe. "Is that like, perhaps meaning 'yes later' or is that more like your 'maybe' when the girls ask you for spending money?" Paula looked at Dennis, the grin on his face was delightful, like a kid opening presents at Christmas. Did they have the time? She wondered. Nope, it would most certainly make them run late. Paula patted him on the cheek "Later, maybe." She replied grinning as she explored the closet for some matching shoes.

Mornings were often like this, the fun of waking up next to the man you love, the chaos of breakfast with the 'terrible twins' and rushing out the door to work. For Paula work was more like play, her antique restoration studio was the third love of her life after Dennis and the girls. Hours a day spent pottering away trying to remove decades of neglect and abuse from items of beauty. Only to have the gut wrenching pain of having to let them go when they sold. In a way, each piece that left the studio was a reminder of the baby boy she never got to hold.

For Dennis, work was lecturing at the University where they had first met. Paula still felt slightly guilty that they met when he was her professor and she the student. At least they had not 'officially' dated until after her masters were conferred. She was not sure she could have managed the degree without the help and encouragement of 'Prof Dennis' as the twins used to call him. He had taken her under his wing and encouraged her to soar to heights she had never thought possible.

First a degree and then onto her masters in History. Dennis had helped her get her bearings, while constantly reminding her what was of most importance in her life, the girls. He was like a compass to her in her storm filled life. Paula remembered back to that fateful day when she called into Professor Farley's study. She had gone to hand her withdrawal form in, as the work, study, and childcare had just got too much. Dennis had almost got angry with her, telling her that she was going to waste her life on anything less than doing what she loved. He had insisted on talking about it further over coffee. It was on this first non-date that he learned about the twins, Gina and Stephanie, and the financial difficulties Paula was facing trying to study, work and raise two little girls. Like most men, Dennis liked to fix things and hated to see women cry. A few calls and a couple of days later he had arranged an emergency scholarship, and Paula's place at Ede was re-established. Dennis may have got her the break, but Paula was the one to prove his faith was not misguided. Working harder than she believed possible, Paula turned in exceptional work, gaining first her degree than her masters. Paula liked to tell Dennis he was her nerdy knight in shining armour.

Dennis, on the other hand, had always thought he got the better part of the deal. Paula was the only woman who had ever managed to get him out of his shell. She was bright, full of humour, loyal to a tee, and came with the two most adorable little girls he had ever met. Although he was tall and quite handsome, Dennis was shy, reserved and preferred the quiet life and his books. Just talking one-on-one to women sent him off into cold sweats. But with Paula it was different. She brought life and love and, to be honest, a bit of chaos to his very ordered life.

Oh, and how that life had changed. He often wondered what Paula saw in him. The twins treated him like he was their biological father. Dennis grinned thinking about the twin tornados that were ‘his' girls. Gina and Stephanie were like peas in a pod. They looked the same, had the same mannerisms, their voices even sounded the same but both Paula and Dennis they could tell them apart. That skill was one that their teachers had not yet mastered.

Yesterday being a case in point. The girls had swapped classes again. Dennis grinned to himself; it was their secret, the one where he was called into the dean's office again only to have to identify each child so they could be sent back to class, the correct class. If Paula found out about this latest event all three of them would be toast. Paula had been quite clear on what she thought about this prank when it had happened the first time. Gina and Steph thought the game was tremendous fun, so this latest thing would probably go on till they got bored of it. The girls did not just have to thank their mother for their looks but also their stubbornness as well. Yes, sir, Dennis thought to himself, it was never dull in the Farley home, and it never ceased to amaze him how much he liked the whirlwind chaos his three girls contained and often released into the world.

Breakfast used to be a simple affair, pry the girls off a children's television show and feed them some form of highly processed breakfast cereal or toast. But now they were teenagers all that had changed. Paula's stubborn streak had devised a three-stage process to rouse the teens from their ‘beauty sleep'. Stage one was the opening of bedroom doors and telling the girls to get up.

When this failed, as it usually did, Paula moved on to step two. This involved opening the curtains to let the bright light of morning cascade in or, if it were still winter, switching on the bedroom lights. However, the girls were as stubborn as their mother and would bury their heads under the covers, leading Paula to stage three. Stage three was the threat of a cold glass of water from the refrigerator. Mostly the threat was enough to have the two teens sitting at the table for breakfast. What was clear to Dennis was that none of his girls were morning people. In fact, straight out of bed, the three of them looked quite frightful, a thought Dennis had quickly learned to keep to himself.

This morning, Dennis focused on tying his necktie as he heard Paula using stages one and two in quick succession. Perhaps today would not be such a chaotic start, he thought. With his necktie complete and a last look in the mirror he made his way to the kitchen. "Morning Dad," groaned two voices in unison, as he entered the kitchen.

The twins' hair looked like birds had nested and Dennis pitied the hairbrushes that had to sort that mess out. They might be physically up, but they were not fully awake Dennis thought. "You two look like you have sat through one of your father's lectures." Paula quipped as she closed the refrigerator door. "Mum!" came two voices again in unison. "So, you have school athletics today then. Are you going to break records this year?" Dennis asked. "I don't think we can Dad, our leg is sore," Gina said while limping towards the toaster.

Paula stopped buttering her toast, "What do you mean 'our' leg is sore? Use proper English; you should say my leg is sore," she replied. "But that's the point!" said Stephanie, "We both have a sore leg, it's both of our left legs, so 'our' leg is sore!" The speaking in the singular had become more frequent of late, and it was one of those things that annoyed Paula about having twins. Why oh why did everything have to involve both of them? Paula thought to herself.

"So which one of you hurt your leg?" Paula had noticed from and early age that if one of the twins got hurt the other 'thought', she was in pain as well. At first, when the girls were infants Paula found it cute, but over time it just got frustrating. She and Dennis were forever trying to work out which child had got injured and which one was psychosomatic. "Not me," said Gina. "Well, don't look at me, and it happened just this morning while we were still in bed" added Stephanie, getting annoyed.

"Stop right there you two, if you think you are going to start an argument over something utterly silly this early in the morning, you can forget it!" replied Paula, forestalling the looming debate. Dennis quietly folded his paper hoping to make a safe exit. "No Dennis, you don't get out of this either," Paula said, shooting Dennis a look that would make a hardened criminal beg for mercy. "You can write the girls a note for athletics."

Dennis hid his relief, at least this did not mean a trip to the doctors. "And" Paula continued while punctuating her point in the air with the butter covered knife she had been using, "If their 'leg' has not got better by the end of school you can take them to the after-hours medical centre." "Great!" thought Dennis, the possibility of 'maybe later' was looking less and less likely. So much for the no-chaos start to the day.

4

Greenspan - Texas

James Kirkland hobbled into the kitchen. "What happened to you?" Dr Kirkland demanded. "I tripped over when I went on my training run. It's not too bad." James replied knowing that this would not satisfy his father. "Not too bad? I will be the judge of that. Did you become a Doctor overnight?" Kirkland demanded. "No" replied James. Dr. Kirkland looked over his glasses at James, "No what?" he barked. "No Sir," said James. Dr. Kirkland folded his newspaper and placed it on the table, "Don't forget your manners James, now let me look at that leg."

James moved around to his father's side of the table and pulled the left leg of his track pants up revealing a large graze. "Hmm…" Kirkland muttered "Did the track coach look at it at all? Even a blind man could see this needs a dressing." "He offered Sir, but I told him I was ok," James said defending one of the nicer teachers at Greenspan High. "Well, he should know better. You are living proof that teenagers have no common sense. I have half a mind to go in with you and see Mrs Jones." James inwardly groaned, that was just the last thing he and Coach Davidson needed.

The Principal Mrs Jones was a battle-axe, she towered over nearly anyone both in height and sheer will. Dr Kirkland was about the only people she spoke kindly to and that was only because the Kirkland's were probably the most wealthy family with a kid at Greenspan High. The principal was feared, but not respected, by the student body. Her wardrobe seemed to consist only of strange full-length knitted dresses accented with multiple strands of brightly coloured beads. Mrs Jones was a chain smoker who believed that only the staff knew she smoked. To hide the smell she would spray herself with so much perfume that she would leave a vapour trail everywhere, she went.

The kids at school use to say that you could hear ‘the Jones' coming by the jingling of the beads and you could tell where she had been by the smell. James had more than once crossed through a stream of the smell when he was sure 'the Jones' had not been past for at least five minutes. One thing was for sure; the Jones was trouble, both to students summoned to her office and to staff that upset the wealthier parents. Students made fun of her behind her back and tried to stay out of her way whenever possible. There was only one student who did not care one iota what the Jones thought, Ashlie Smith.

Ashlie was in denial and thought that most people were just a waste of oxygen. Society said that because she was a girl, she should act like a girl, Ashlie thought otherwise. It was not that she did not think of herself as female, it was more that she was angry that she was expected to conform. For Ashlie being a girl did not mean she had to be a girly-girl. From her early teens, Ashlie had set out to be her own person, an individual. Her first act of social defiance was to refuse to answer to her name; she would only respond to Ash.

Ashlie's dad Scott, a local detective in the police force, had long since given up fighting the battle of what Ashlie called herself also now called her Ash. About the only person that still called her by her full name was 'the Jones'. Ash's wardrobe was equal to her name and changed with the frequency of the seasons. The current fashion was black - black jeans, black t-shirt with some geeky witty logo or statement that only a sci-fi fan would understand and a black beanie pulled over her short hair. Today's shirt read "I survived the Fire Swamp," a reference to a quote from her favourite chick-flick the Princess Bride.

She carried an air of confidence that many adults twice her age would die for and she cared very little what other people thought. 'The Jones' and Ash clashed on almost a weekly basis, the very fact that Ash was the straight A student but one that did not conform to the Jones idea of what teenagers should be, irked the Principal like nothing else. To Ash 'The Jones', a name she had come up with, was just another 'stiff' trying to force her into a mould. Their latest clash had been over Ash inviting another girl to the school dance. It was not that she felt romantic towards girls, rather she noticed someone not getting asked so invited her instead.

Mrs Jones was horrified and made the point that only boys and girls could partner up for the dance. Ash's actions caused a massive backlash from the real lesbian and gay students that even got reported in the local paper. The Jones was forced back down, facing not only a student revolt but increasing pressure from parents and the school board. Ash and her 'girlfriend' attended but spent the entire night dancing with as many boys as possible. To 'the Jones' it was like a smack in the face.

Ash stopped to look up at what she referred to as the Kirkland mansion. It was by no means the largest house in town, but it had a certain presence. It was two stories, pristine white painted cladding, with cute little flower boxes, towered over those that approached, and the manicured lawns and garden beds almost demanded signs saying to keep off the grass. It sat on a slight rise so that anyone walking to the door felt the presence of the house looming over them. This suited Dr Kirkland just fine; it meant he could get the first word in, usually "Go away we don't want any," or words to that effect. Ash started up the path. Dr Kirkland rarely got the chance to tell Ash to go away, as she either opened the front door and ploughed right in, or if Dr Kirkland had locked the door she would just scale the trellis up to James' bedroom.

She and James had been friends since the Kirkland's had moved in. Ash and her dad lived three houses down but Ash and James' upstairs bedrooms faced one another across the single story roofed houses of the neighbours. Ben, Ash's father, liked James well enough, but the same could not be said of how the Dr Kirkland felt about Ash.

To Dr Kirkland Ash was a threat to everything he had worked for. He did not believe his son should associate with people of 'their' class. Ash couldn't have cared less. James was her friend and to hell with his father. It was like James was adopted. He was the complete opposite of Dr Simon Kirkland. Where Dr Kirkland was focused on outward appearances, James was only interested in people. In fact, there was not even any physical similarity between James and his dad. James was blond and willowy whereas Dr Kirkland was short and squat, more ball shaped to Ash's mind. She often wondered whether James must favour Mrs Kirkland. James' mother had died when he was eight.

Ash and her dad had only just moved to the area, so Ash had never met Mrs Kirkland. Ash figured that James must take after his mother, as it would be impossible for him to turn out to be the good guy he was if both his parents were like Dr Kirkland. Although Ash had lost her mother two, Dr Kirkland did not see the two children as equals and his distaste for Ash was apparent. James was like a brother to Ash and she a sister to him. Neither had other siblings, so it was natural for them to gravitate towards each other.

The early teenage years had caused many of their peers to question, mostly behind their backs, if Ash and James were an item. Those with the courage to ask them directly were explicitly told it was just friends. In time the rumours evaporated, and even Dr Kirkland seemed to be resigned to the friendship publicly and was secretly relieved it had become nothing more.

Today the door to the Kirkland 'Manor' was not a barrier to Ash's entry. Ash opened the door and breezed past Dr Kirkland with nothing more than a "Hey, Mr K," as she made her way upstairs to James' room. Ash could feel the annoyed look Dr Kirkland gave her behind her back as she went past and it gave her no small measure of pleasure.

"Hey stud," Ash said having opened the door and gone right in. "Whoa, I'm trying to get dressed here, can't a guy get some privacy?" James was partially dressed in blue denim jeans but had not yet got a top on. "Oh like I haven't seen it all before," Ash stated as she admired the fine looking form before her. Just because she did not have romantic feelings for James didn't mean she could not look and approve of what she saw. James was limping and favouring his leg. "What happen to you?" Ash asked pointing at the limp. "Took a fall during training this morning, it's fine." James shrugged. "Has the old man seen it?" Ash asked. James nodded. "How did that go?"

James sighed, "About as well as you would expect, says he's going to go down the school and rail on Coach Davidson. Probably won't if I stop limping by tomorrow. It's not like he is going to go out of his way to do it. That would make it look like he cares." James said.

"Yea, I hope coach doesn't catch it from him or worse if your dad goes to the Jones. The coach will never hear the end of it then." Ash replied, "Coach Davidson, you really must put the safety of the school's athletes ahead of your personal desires for success." Ash mimicked in her very best Jones voice. James was in fits laughing; Ash could mimic almost anyone, and she had the Jones down perfectly.

"Hey, I think I saw a full-length knitted dress at the second-hand store, I could get it for you and some beads, if you want to have a look and the voice?" he offered. "Oh, is that what does it for you 'Jamesie,' would that make you love me?" Ash teased batting her eyes at James. "Please, no, anything but that!" James said finishing the sentence by pretending to be sick.

"So what about little miss redhead? I watched you two at lunch the other day, is she the one then?" James love life was a constant fascination to Ash. "Hmm, a possibility but I think she's into shopping, and I am not sure I'm ready for that level of commitment. She has got a killer smile and looking at those red locks sure makes my heart race..." James was unable to finish the sentence as his pillow socked him square in the face. This was the first move of an epic pillow war with the crazy goth chick from down the road. Yes, James thought to himself after he collapsed against the side of the bed ten minutes later, having Ash around made him feel like he was more than the just brag point for his father. She made him feel that he might just matter to someone. After his mum had died James had become very close to Ash while his father continued maintaining his distance.

5

Simon Kirkland sat in his home study. The door was locked as he started up his computer to update a file that he had begun so many years before. When this started he had committed this part of his practice to a notebook, but that had long been replaced by a file on a floppy disk, then a hard drive, and now a secure USB memory stick. The old items had been confined to the safe located behind the family painting hanging behind his desk, but the file he was updating still contained three years of very sensitive material.

If it were ever to be found and revealed, he would lose everything he had worked for. It all started in the sixties, and it had taken a brilliant mind like his to conceive of the plan. Kirkland chuckled to himself, 'Conceived,' yes that was an excellent pun. Each and every entry in the notebook, floppy disk, hard disk and computer file began with conceived.

Kirkland's idea was simple. Women were often coming to see him with a problem, they were often pregnant with multiples, twins and triplets even one set of quads once, and he was an expert in multiple pregnancies. The woman would come to have Dr Kirkland help them deliver their bundles of joy. His professional services did not come cheap, and the women and their husbands often paid hundreds of dollars to have their children delivered. But hundreds of dollars paled in comparison to the real money.

That came from selling babies to wealthy couples who could not have children. It didn't matter to Kirkland if they could not conceive naturally or that they didn't want to have the inconvenience of pregnancy, let alone the pain of delivery. As long as they would pay, then Dr Kirkland was happy to provide his unique service.

The plan was almost fool proof. When Dr Kirkland had a prospective client, he waited until a mother came in with a multiple pregnancy. On the day of delivery, the mother would have to have an urgent general anaesthetic. Kirkland would tell her one of her babies was in distress, and he needed to operate now. After recovering, she would be told that not all of her babies had survived. Very few mothers got to see the 'dead' babies as they were told that either the baby was too deformed or that it had already been destroyed. Only once had the plan almost unravelled when the mother was insistent on seeing her deformed baby. As luck would have it, there was a deformed dead baby in the morgue from another mother. This baby was shown to the mother, and she even cradled it for a period before the nurse insisted that they take it away.

The system worked for two main reasons. Kirkland only accepted expectant mothers with good health, and this lowered the chances of a baby dying for real, thus keeping his mortality rates very similar to those of his colleagues and second, he was never greedy only ever doing three or four 'adoptions' per year at the most. There were risks, of course, staff had to be paid to look the other way, a cost that was naturally passed onto the buyers. Sometimes he even had to pay a staff member to be quiet after they got cold feet. Nurse Samantha Scott was one such case, and she had been party to Kirkland's riskiest steal to date, the teenager he called his son. Nurse Scott had been paid handsomely at the time, plus a "keep your mouth shut" bonus when she left nursing. As an extra bit of insurance

Kirkland had sent some private muscle over to make sure Nurse Scott had got the message about what would happen if she blabbed. Kirkland was confident that the loose end called Samantha Scott was neatly tied up.

Olivia had begged him to get her a baby boy. It was a constant tension in his life. A bit like how the builder's house is never finished, the OB/GYN's wife having no baby. In the end, he gave in. He had never really wanted the boy and now that Olivia was gone, he was saddled with him. At least James performed well. Hell, the kid excels at pretty much everything he does. Kirkland thought to himself. It never entered his mind that James got his talent from his natural parents.

Simon entered the latest adoption into the file and saved it checking the encryption was working before switching to his shadow internet banking account in the Cayman Islands. Yes, there it was, $375,000 deposited by the adopting parents. Kirkland smiled to himself; the abortion lobby groups had been the best thing for business. Overnight the number of legitimate adoptable babies had dried up. His was a business that could only go in one direction, up. Opening his humidor, Kirkland lit up his only personal vice, a Lonsdale's Cigar of Saint Luis Rey. It was a vice he only ever indulged in after a successful ‘heist'.

6

Jan 19, 2013

Paula sat in the outdoor seating area. The weather was calm but cold. Paula preferred it out here. There were two reasons she liked Alfonzo's Coffee shop. The first was they served her coffee in a big mug, just the way she liked it. Her second was the outdoor seating looked out across the road at the basketball courts at the local high school. Her personal secret, she liked to look at the young men playing ball. This was not some weird fantasy, rather a time for her to imagine what her lost baby boy might have been like. She did not believe that any particular kid on the court was her lost son. Rather she was searching for what it might feel like to have a boy child there with them. She watched as they parried and sparred for the ball and she could almost feel herself on the sideline cheering for his team. Often, as she watched, a tear would roll down her cheek.

Samantha Scott looked out from the indoor area at Paula and noticed the tears. Looking past Paula, it was obvious to Sam what was causing Paula's grief. Each day that Paula bought her coffee was a constant reminder of what she had done all those years ago., a knife being twisted in her conscience. Damn it; Sam cursed under her breath, this job was meant to take her mind off her past life. "There is nothing like a busy hand to keep a wandering mind in check," her grandfather would always say. Sam could only imagine what he would say if he knew what she had done, what she had been a part of.

Sam's newly found faith in Jesus was about the only thing keeping her in one piece. Oh God, I need your strength today, she prayed. It was going to be now or never. "Tracey, you want to take the inside tables for a while?" Sam asked her co-worker. The cold kept most of the customers, inside meaning fewer tips for working the outside tables. Sam was handing over the chance for Tracey to make more than serving the external clients. "Totally," Tracey beamed. "Cool, I'll go and see if some of them want a refill."

Sam moved outside, clearing some empty cups to steady her nerves. Approaching Paula's table the nerves got the better of her. The cups seemed to leap off her tray crashing to the ground. The sound jarred Paula out of her daydream. "Oh, I'm so sorry," Sam said bending down to pick up the broken cups and mugs. "Here, let me help you," Paula replied. Both women bent down and began to pick up the pieces. "You know," Paula said, "you look familiar, I am sure we have met somewhere before." "Oh," stammered Samantha, "I usually work the inside tables, but I have seen you out here every few days," Samantha stalled for time, she desperately needed to get her composure back. "That must be it. I must have seen you out here," Paula replied.

As Paula sat back in her chair, she looked at the woman picking up the last pieces. Somewhere deep in her mind, a memory stirred, but she could not hold on to it. Paula frowned at her inability to remember. No, something was off, the waitress looked nervous, and she was now sure she had seen her before, but where?

Samantha picked up the remaining pieces and asked if Paula would like another coffee. "No thanks," replied

Paula, "Just the bill please." Samantha nodded and took the broken cups back to the counter to prepare the bill. "Hey, Tracey?" Samantha asked. "Yeah, what's up to Sam, you have a drop?" Tracey motioning to the broken cups. "Yes, I don't think I feel so good. Can you cover the rest of my shift?" she asked. "Hey, no prob, You ok? It's a bit quiet today anyway, you go home and have a rest and leave this to Super Tracey," she replied. "Thanks, I will just take that lady's bill out, and then I'll be on my way."

Sam gathered up her bag and Paula's bill and went back outside. Laying the folded bill on the table, Samantha dug deep and used what was possibly the last ounce of courage she had left. "Here's the cheque Miss. Johnson," she said using Paula's maiden name. If Paula had noticed the use of her maiden name, she made no reference to it. "Thank you," Paula replied, watching as Samantha headed off to her car. Samantha was developing a massive headache, she hoped she had done the right thing, but only time would tell.

7

Paula opened the folded bill for her coffee and muffin from earlier. Folded neatly within was a second piece of paper. She opened it, wondering if it were some discount or special off her next cup of coffee. What she read made the blood drain from her face. For the first time, it felt like the cold outside had seeped into her veins. Paula hurriedly looked around for the waitress but could not see her anywhere.

Tucking the second piece of paper in her bag, she made her way inside to pay. While paying her bill, Paula enquired where the other waitress was that had served her. Tracey replied that she had not been feeling well so had gone home. Paula handed over the money and thanked her. She was still shaky as she walked back to her car. Once inside Paula removed the piece of paper. Her hands were trembling as she reread the note.

"Your son did not die at birth, he is alive, and I can help you find him. Meet me at the central park by the fountain at 4 pm."

It was signed, Nurse Samantha Scott.

Paula's heart pounded in her chest. "My baby is alive!" It seemed too crazy to be true. She looked at her watch, 2:20 pm, did she have time to see Dennis before the meeting? It would be close; she would just have to chance it. Starting the car, she drove across town to Ede University. Would Dennis be free, or stuck in lectures?

Paula was so unsure, the details of the note kept repeating through her mind. Dennis would help, but she needed to see him, to show him, she needed his support, now more than ever before. The horn from a car snapped her back to the present as she sped through a red light. Paula buttoned off the throttle, and the engine sound of her VW Golf returned to a more regular cadence.

The entrance to the University came into view. Parking seemed to be pretty easy for 3 pm on a Tuesday. Dennis' schedule become clear in her mind once more - no lectures on Tuesday afternoons. Pulling into a park, Paula jumped out of the car, almost forgetting to grab the note from Samantha. Dennis' office was on the second floor of the old grey stone building. The ceilings were high and the walls lined with darkly stained wood panels. The old chipped linoleum floors and the flaking paint that often annoyed her were forgotten as she sped up the stairs to his office. Not even knocking Paula opened the door and went in.

Dennis was sitting behind his desk. There were piles of papers that Paula assumed were midterms for marking covering most of the surface. Lining his study walls were old wooden bookcases filled with books all relating to Dennis' love of History. Dennis looked up and a smile that began to form on seeing his wife was quickly replaced with a look of concern. "Paula, what's wrong?" he asked, rising from his desk and coming to her. Paula was breathless, "He's alive… She called me by my maiden name, my babies alive! I didn't recognise her at the time, and I didn't even realise she had used my maiden name until I went to drive off. I knew I had seen her before, but I couldn't place her, I mean it's not like she was working in a coffee shop the last time I saw her." Part sentences tumbled out of Paula like a machine gun spitting bullets. "Whoa, slow down champ," Dennis gathered Paula into his arms in a hug, "Let's start at the beginning, can we?

Paula took a big breath, "Dennis, the baby boy I lost when I had the twins, I mean the triplets?" "Yes," Dennis replied with more of a question than an answer. "He is alive, he didn't die," Paula explained. Confusion clouded Dennis's face, "What, how, wait a moment," Dennis was trying to keep up, "the baby boy, your little boy is alive? Are you sure? How do you know?"

Paula began to pace the office, a sure sign she was upset, "I was over at Alfonzo's having a coffee and a bite to eat, I think I go there to look over at the basketball courts, and sometimes I imagine what it would have been like if he had lived." Dennis closed in and hugged Paula again he held his tongue as this was one of those 'let your woman talk' moments. He was learning another side of this amazing lady, and although it hurt to know she had kept this secret from him, he could see the pain she had carried in her eyes. Tears were running down Paula's face now, and like a little girl she wiped them away with the corner of her sleeve, mimicking the time when she had been told of her baby boy's death so many years ago. Paula continued to pace the room, "I recognised the waitress but couldn't place where I knew her from. It seemed she was nervous about something and dropped a whole heap of cups. After she had picked them up, she returned with my bill, and she called me Miss Johnson!"

Dennis still did not have the full picture, but knowing that pushing for details would not help he remained silent. "I opened the bill, and this was folded inside." Paula handed the note to Dennis. Walking to his desk, Dennis picked up his glasses and sat down to read the note. Questions swirled through Dennis's mind, "Who is she, how could she know the boy survived, it seems too fantastic to believe." Dennis replied, after reading the note.

"She was my nurse at the hospital. It was Samantha who told me Daniel had died. I asked to see him, but they said he was severely deformed." A small gasp came from Paula as she realised she had just used his name for the first time since he had died. Dennis crossed over to her again. "You're going to this meeting?" Dennis replied with more of a statement than a question. "Yes, I have to know. Will you come with me? I don't think I can do this on my own." Paula sniffed up and wiped another tear from her face. "I would not let you do it on your own." Dennis took her hand "You know it could be some trick or extortion thing," Dennis said in the most gentle way possible.

"I know, but I have to find out…" her voice trailed off "But if I don't know for certain then I will always be wondering if it was true." Dennis decided that now was the time to take charge, "If we are going to meet this woman at four then we better be going, it's 3:25 pm now." Grabbing his keys and his jacket that was hanging on the back of his chair, Dennis ushered Paula out of his office towards the car park.

8

Samantha was sick to her stomach, waves of nausea threatened to expel her lunch. She paced backwards and forwards in front of the park bench. What was she doing, if Dr Kirkland ever found out, well things could go very badly for her, she thought, doubt creeping into her mind? Perhaps now was the time for a new start, move somewhere Kirkland would not have any influence.

But Dr Kirkland would find out. Now that Paula Johnson knew the truth or at least even a small part of the truth she would not stop until she had all the answers. The sudden realisation of what she had done caused Sam to turn and vomit into the bushes behind the park bench she was waiting on. She did not feel any better but was pleased that no one had seen her lose her dignity. Perhaps Paula would not come; maybe Paula had not seen the note.

With her hopes raised, she looked around the park. The only people she saw were a man and a woman. They were walking hand in hand but still a way off in the distance. Samantha thought they must be feeling the cold as they seemed to be advancing with a purpose. As they drew near Sam was surprised to discover that the woman was Paula. The man holding her hand was obviously her husband or partner. Sam inwardly groaned, "Damn, this just got harder," she told herself.

Paula and Dennis walked towards the only woman they could see. It was clear that she had not seen their approach, as they saw Samantha stand up and vomit into the bushes behind a bench. "This must be hard for her," Dennis stated. Paula's grip tightened on Dennis's hand, "Well it's about to get much more challenging." There was steel in Paula's voice; the shock had been replaced by anger and the mother lion was about to bare her teeth. Dennis sensed Paula's building rage and decided it would do more harm than good to vent right now. Now was the time for answers not accusations.

The anger could come later if this were all legit. Samantha had noticed them now as they walked up towards her. Dennis gave Paula's hand a quick squeeze, and leaning in whispered: "I know you're angry, but you need information, not vengeance, right now you must calm down." Paula wanted to scream, at Dennis, at Samantha, at the world. But Dennis was only trying to calm her down she realised. "I'll work on it," she said between gritted teeth. "But I want to smack her in the face." They approached Samantha.

"Ms Johnson, I'm Samantha Scott. I was the nurse at your children's birth." Samantha said holding out her hand. Paula ignored the offered hand, "It's Mrs Farley now, and this is my husband Dennis." Paula replied with ice in her voice. Samantha looked directly at Paula, "I am so sorry, I never meant to hurt you, I thought we were doing you a favour. A girl so young with three small babies, no husband, it would have been terrible, you would never have coped." Sam's voice trailed off as she heard the conviction leave her voice.

Paula glared at Sam for what seemed like a lifetime. Dennis cleared his throat, "You mean it's true; you took Paula's baby boy?" he asked, clearly in shock. Sam nodded.

"Where is he Samantha?" demanded Paula "Where's my son?"

The stress of the moment finally got to Sam and the world went fuzzy as she collapsed in a heap on the ground. "Oh crap," muttered Dennis as he scooped her up. "What on earth do we do now?" he asked. "We take her home; I still have a heap of questions that need answers." Paula was still ticked off. Dennis turned to Paula, "You mean we're not taking her straight to the police?" he asked, shock showing on his face. Paula stayed her ground, "No way, she goes in there, and a lawyer will be telling her to keep her mouth shut faster than my temper. No, she's coming home with us until I get some information." Paula replied. Dennis was looking quite concerned, "But that's kidnapping, Paula! Just because she might have stolen your son doesn't make it ok to kidnap her." Dennis was the one getting angry now.

Sam had started to come to, "No it's ok I will go with you. I have to tell you about your son," she insisted. Paula turned and started back to the car, "Right back to the car then," she ordered. Paula was in charge, and she would be damned if her husband or the bitch that stole her son were going to get in her way now. The three of them headed back to Paula's VW with Dennis supporting Sam as she was still a bit wobbly on her feet. "This sometimes happens when I have not had enough to eat," Sam explained. "Well, we will all have a bite to eat and a warm drink back at our place," Dennis replied, "And a nice long talk." Paula hissed out between clenched teeth.

During the drive to the Farley's home, neither woman spoke. Paula had insisted on sitting next to Sam in the back seat. Insurance, she thought, in case Sam made a break for it. Dennis had to squeeze his tall frame into the tiny driver's seat of Paula's little VW Golf. As they drove, Dennis chatted away about the weather, his work, and the twins. All the while Paula glared at him in the rear view mirror.

Paula knew Dennis was trying to keep things on an even keel, but right now she just wanted to sock someone. The woman sitting next to her was her primary target, but her husband in the driver's seat might just have to do. The drive to the Farley's was thankfully only twenty minutes as traffic was light. Samantha admired the tree-lined avenue; the mainly single story homes sat comfortably in their established gardens. The trees lining the street would look amazing when they had their leaves come spring, Samantha thought.

As Dennis slowed to turn up a driveway, Samantha's heart had sunk into the pit of her stomach. Dennis stopped in front of a double garage door that was connected to a tidy but modern single story home and had to fish around the glove compartment for the garage door remote. What is he doing? Paula thought, We never park this car in the garage. Paula suddenly realised that Dennis was going to ensure Samantha could not run off by closing the garage door before exiting the car. I love you, Dennis! Was all Paula could think right then, her aggression towards him evaporating in an instant.

To Sam, the clanging sound of the garage door closing was like someone shutting the door on a prison cell. She was in it neck deep now, and who knew how this would end. Sam unbuckled and climbed out of the car. She took the time to have a look around the garage. It was clean and mostly tidy. Two mountain bikes hung from individual hoists on one side of the room while two hoists remained empty, probably for the twin girls' bikes she surmised. On the other side four canoe or kayak things, Sam never could remember the difference, hung lined up in a neat row. They must enjoy the outdoors she thought. Dennis opened a door that Sam realised must lead through to the house. Paula led the way, with Sam following and Dennis bring up the rear. They walked down a hallway, the only open door revealing a laundry room with two washing baskets overflowing with what looked like teenage girls clothing.

Paula led them through to the kitchen, and plonking her bag down on the kitchen counter she took a seat at a circular table at one end of the room. The kitchen was clean but chaotic. In the centre unmatched pots and pans hung over an island counter. A small bunch of flowers sat in the middle of the table giving the room colour and warmth. Hanging on the walls were framed family photographs. It was a record of a family, holidays, fun times, kids playing under a sprinkler. The pictures anchored the family to this space. This was a room where family met; Sam could image the conversations, the arguments, and laughter that this room had witnessed. This was not simply a house, but a home. A part of Sam deeply yearned for this kind of life and all that came with it. Sam's apartment was in stark contrast to what she saw here.

Dennis dropped the car keys into a bowl on the kitchen counter and took a seat next to his wife. Samantha pulled out a chair opposite Paula and Dennis and sat down. "You probably have lots of questions, but perhaps I should start at the beginning?" she asked.

"That would be a good idea," Dennis replied as he held Paula's hand. Sam realised that she had been wrong, Paula wasn't weak, she was strong, and with Dennis by her side, she became formidable. Not in a bad way, more in an unspoken You mess with mine, you mess with me. Oh, how Sam had misjudged her so badly all those years ago.

"Ok, I'm just going to come out with it. I was paid to look the other way when Dr Kirkland stole babies and sold them to other couples." Paula gasped and was squeezing Dennis's hand hard enough to hurt. "Dr Kirkland would select a pregnant woman who was carrying twins or triplets, and during the labour, we would fake a medical emergency. In your case, we told you we could not hear one of the babies heartbeats. We were then able to put the patient to sleep with a general anaesthetic. When the patient came to after the c-section we told them one of their babies had died. The child we took was then sold to wealthy families who said they could not conceive. "Dennis was shocked, "Surely the mothers would ask to see their dead babies?" The question was as much for Paula as it was for Sam. Paula looked down at her hands, "I asked, they told me he was terribly deformed and I just believed them," Paula sobbed. "We only ever took babies from solo Mums; I thought we were helping them," Samantha tried to explain.

"Helping me! You think stealing my baby was helping me? How sick are you? You take my baby, and you think it helps?" Paula shouted she was on her feet, her hands gripping the edge of the table and her knuckles were turning white. Samantha swallowed, "I know, I must look like a monster to you. I was only involved on two occasions, and then I could not do it anymore. I got out Dr Kirkland and threatened me if I ever talked I would get it…" Sam's voice trailed off.

"Samantha, what changed, why have you now told us?" Dennis was beginning to see how dangerous the situation was that Sam was in. "About a year ago I started attending a church. I know it sounds like a canned answer, but I needed to fix this if I was ever going to have peace. I tried to find you but I couldn't, you had disappeared. Six months ago I started working at the coffee shop and then one day you just walked in," Sam explained. "You believe in God?" Paula asked in a soft voice. "I do, but I am not sure He believes in me," Sam replied. "Who has Paula's baby, Samantha?" Dennis asked. Sam realised she had not said, "Oh, of course, you don't know. Dr Kirkland and his wife have him; they called him James. Your baby was the only one they kept." There was suddenly a big thumping sound that came from down in the garage. "Drat, the girls, are home," Dennis exclaimed.

9

It was a study day, and Gina and Steph had stayed later at school to get some quiet time to study in the library. It was not that home was not quiet, it just felt right to study surrounded by walls of books. As they rode their bikes back, they joked and laughed about the day's antics. Today had been a day back in their regular classes. Dad had warned them that if they switch again, he would tell mum, even if it meant dobbing himself in as well. The switch classes prank never seemed to get old, and in fact was often used at the beginning of the new term or class. Teachers had even tried to keep them in the same class for a while, thinking that would somehow make it easier. Well, it did make it easier but not for the teachers.

Like two peas in a pod to look at, the twins could not be more unalike in personality. Gina had a bent towards the arts. Her life revolved around photography, in particular, sports photography. Her camera bag hardly ever left her side and all her pocket money was spent on getting new gear or prints of her latest shoots. Stephanie was the joker out of the two. If there was a mad plan to be hatched, you could be sure that Steph was the one behind it. Steph's crazy plans almost never left Gina out, so she was not the only one getting in trouble. Early on Paula had discovered that both girls were extremely competitive and used this as a way of controlling her 'Firecracker Twins'. Chuck them at a sport together, and bang, the battle for dominance would begin. Cycling was the latest thing. It was not just a form of transport; it was a reason to race, to compete.

The twins raced their bikes up the drive, their sudden breaking leaving tire marks on the pavement. Steph grinned at Gina, "I guess I won." She stated. "In your dreams. You cut me off." Gina replied. Both girls were short of breath but still managed to laugh as they wheeled their bikes around to the side door of the garage and let themselves in. "That's weird," Gina remarked, "mum's parked in the garage." The girls attached their bikes to the hoists and, inevitably, raced to see who could pull them up to the ceiling faster. As usual, both bikes crashed into the ceiling at almost the same time with an audible thump. "Oops," Steph grinned, "hope mum didn't hear that." With that, the girls opened the door to the house and went in.

Samantha turned towards the noise as two teenage girls stepped into the kitchen. "Hello," both Gina and Steph said in perfect unison. "Oh, um, good afternoon," Sam managed in reply. The twins were completely identical. It was like looking in a mirror. Sam had no idea how anyone could tell these two apart. They were about average height with long brown hair and they looked quite athletic. "Girls, we need a little privacy for a bit. Would you go up…" Dennis was interrupted by Paula, "no Dennis, this involves them as much as it does us. They need to hear this."

"Mum," Gina began to explain, "it was just a prank," Steph cut in to finish off the sentence "No one was hurt, and we didn't have a test or anything." Paula's ‘mother of twins' instincts kicked into overdrive. "You switched places again?" she demanded. Gina replied, "It's fine, Dad came in and sorted it out, I don't know why they sent someone to speak to you at home." Dennis was trying to make the cut signal without Paula seeing until she turned to him mid-gesture. Paula looked at Dennis, "You knew about this?" she asked, her anger was reaching epic proportions. Dennis needed to steer the conversation back to Samantha. "Um, girls, this lady, her name is Samantha. She is not here from school." Dennis was desperate to return the attention to Samantha rather than his trip to the principal's office. "Come and sit down while I make some drinks," Dennis suggested hoping to avoid any further confrontation.

Gina and Stephanie sat down at the table, picking a seat each side of their mother. Something about this meeting was not right, and with the obvious tension in the air, they protectively bracketed Paula. Sam was again stunned by this family. It was like each had strength but faced with a challenge or threat they united and became an even stronger unit. "Samantha, these are our girls, Gina," Paula indicated to her left, "and Stephanie," who was on her right. "I think you have some news for my girls, don't you Samantha?" Paula phrased this more like a statement than a question, and Samantha knew an implied test when she saw one.

Gina and Steph looked over at Samantha, both thinking what on earth was going on. "Girls, I was the nurse that helped your mother give birth, and I was also part of a lie that involved stealing your baby brother from your mum and giving him to another family. Your brother didn't die; he was taken from your family." Dennis looked over from boiling the kettle. Paula had calmed down as he expected she would, given time. Just the act of forcing Samantha to tell the twins was enough for Paula to feel like she was back in control. He glanced at Gina and Steph to gauge their reaction to the news. All three adults in the room were shocked by their response.

Gina and Steph at first looked stunned then confused. Suddenly Steph grinned, looking at Gina, "The leg!" she exclaimed. Gina got it at the same time, "Yes, the leg, the sore leg! I guess it finally makes sense." Gina replied. "And before you say it, no, we have not gone mad," Paula had started to say something. "No," Gina replied, "don't you get it? All those times that Steph and I got a pain or sick and you could not find a cause? It's just like when Steph gets hurt, and I feel pain where she felt it. We are feeling his pain." Paula slowly nodded, crazy as this day was, she began to see the logic of what the twins were saying.

Sam could hardly believe what she was hearing. "Do you mean to tell me you feel each other's pain?" she asked, beginning to get what the twins were saying. "They always have," replied Paula, shaking her head, "It is freaky, but then there were other times when they would claim that neither of them had tripped or fallen, but the pain was there. When was the last time Dennis?" she asked. "Um must have been about two weeks ago as far as I can remember. When they were complaining about a sore leg?" Dennis replied as he brought over a tray with cups and the steaming kettle. Paula nodded, "Yes that was it. Dennis took them to the doctor, and he couldn't find anything," she recounted.

No one spoke as they each poured themselves a hot drink until Samantha spoke up. "I suppose you will want to call the Police now." Paula looked at Dennis, and some form of communication passed between them, "Where is he, Samantha? I mean where does he live?" Samantha was shocked; she thought that this would be the moment where the police would be called and then all hell would break loose. "Texas, Greenspan, Texas. The Kirkland's shifted their practice there about ten years ago; I think local people here might have started to suspect things were a bit off.

Dennis looked over at his wife; he could see her thinking. "Samantha, it took considerable courage to come and tell us, how many babies do you think Dr Kirkland has stolen? Paula asked. "I'm not sure; I believe he has been at it for ages. He used to brag that they did at least three or four a year." Sam replied. "That doesn't seem like many," commented Dennis. "Dr Kirkland didn't want to do too many as people might suspect something was amiss." Sam went on, "I don't know how much they paid him, but I was paid $10,000 for each baby, to keep my mouth shut. Who knows what he paid the other theatre staff," she replied.

Gina looked at them all at the table, "If this Dr Kirkland guy has been selling babies ever since we were born then there are heaps of kids not with their real parents," she exclaimed. "Did Dr Kirkland keep any records?" Dennis asked. "I think he must have, but the first sign of the police I am sure he will ditch the evidence," Sam replied. "I am not certain how this can be undone." Paula looked at Dennis who nodded, "I don't think sending you to the police is the best option." Paula announced, "no, I believe that it would be better to have you on our side if we need you." Samantha looked straight at Paula. "Mrs Farley, I want to promise you that no matter what happens I am on your side and I will do anything or sign anything that helps you get your son back," Samantha promised.

For the next hour, they debated all the options from contacting the police to even kidnapping James back. "This is getting us nowhere," groaned Steph. "I think it would be best if we all slept on this tonight. The path forward might be clearer tomorrow," Dennis announced. The others all agreed. "Well, Samantha, I guess we should un-abduct you and drop you home," said Dennis. They all laughed, and the humour was strangely helpful. "I will drop you home, and we will let you know what we are going to do tomorrow," Dennis said picking up the car keys from the bowl on the countertop. As Sam got up to leave, Paula stood and came over to her. Sam waited for another tirade or even a physical blow. Paula stepped in and gave her a hug, "I forgive you," she quietly said. Paula broke the embrace and left the room, right now she needed some time alone.

10

The drive to Sam's apartment was done mostly in silence, Samantha only speaking to tell Dennis which way to go. Dennis pulled into a park outside Samantha's apartment. "She's still angry at me," Samantha stated. "Yes, but that will not last forever. Paula may have a hot temper, but she is fair. If she said you're forgiven then that's what you are," Dennis replied. Sam looked at Dennis, "People say things like that all the time, but they don't mean it," Sam countered. Dennis turned to face her, "I think you misjudged her sixteen years ago. She has not only survived, but she has thrived, you might just be misjudging her now as well. Get some rest, Sam, it looks like things could get fascinating tomorrow."

Sam hopped out of the car and headed to her apartment. Dennis took a last look at Sam as she walked away. She may have made some mistakes, but she was trying to do the right thing now, and in Dennis's mind, that was a good start.

Gina knocked on Steph's door. "Come in," was Steph's reply. Gina opened the door and walked in. Steph's walls were covered with posters of music groups. Her collection represented an eclectic mix of bands from Mumford and Sons through to Bob Dylan. Gina, on the other hand, had almost no posters on her walls, rather she had enlargements of photos she had taken. She preferred reading over music, and her room was filled with books and bookcases.

"Crazy day huh?" Gina asked as she came in. "The craziest. We have a brother." Steph replied grinning. "So what now?" Gina asked climbing up on Steph's bed. "We could send him a message." Steph replied, "Thought that if we feel his pain then maybe he feels ours." Steph said grinning while pulling out a drawing pin holding up a poster of the band Queen on the wall. "Oh no, you don't," cried Gina "You total nut-bar!" The twins began to wrestle, causing both to laugh fit to kill.

"Hey," came Dennis' voice from the door, "I can help with that, but I think it would be safer to jab you both just in case he only feels the pain from only one of you," he suggested. "Mum!" came a shouted plea from the twins, "Help!" "Don't look to me to sort your wars out. I have enough issues of my own." Paula said as she walked past Steph's door. "Probably a good time to call it night girls," Dennis said, "it has been a tremendous day."

Later in bed, Dennis held Paula as she wept, and even she could not say if the tears were happy or sad. "I have to see him, Dennis, I have to know what he's like, that he happy." "I know love, I understand." Dennis continued to hold Paula until her ragged breaths settled and he could be sure she was asleep. Dennis lay there with his arm around Paula as he dealt with the anger he felt. Someone had hurt his family, and he felt powerless to fix this problem. Not being able to fix things chaffed. If he couldn't fix this himself, then he had to help Paula. Perhaps just seeing the boy would help Paula to move on, yes perhaps that was the answer. Sleep would come for Dennis, but it would take its time tonight. Rather than dwell on all that had happened today he thought of the amazing family he now had.

11

Jan 20, 2013

Dennis awoke to discover he was in bed alone and it was nearly a 'running late' day. Getting up he grabbed a dressing gown and headed down to the kitchen. Sitting at the kitchen table, all three of his girls were talking quietly. Hmm, he thought, plans were afoot. Dennis walked over to the coffee machine and poured himself a large mug. No one said anything while he measured out two spoons of sugar, added milk, and gave it a good stir. He inhaled the aroma of fresh coffee and then took a sip. "Ok, you can tell me your plan now, and don't try to spin me some BS line about not having a plan," Dennis said as he took a chair and sat.

Paula looked at Dennis with a 'who me' look, "How do you know we have a plan?" Paula asked with a twinkle in her eye. "Well, for starters since when are these two up this early and not causing chaos?" he asked pointing at Gina and Steph. Paula had to admit Dennis had a point, unlike him she couldn't bluff even if it were life and death, which was just one reason she never played poker, of any kind, with her husband.

"Ok, so here it is. The girls spent half the night finding just where in Greenspan they live," Paula continued, "they have even managed to find a photo of our boy and..." Dennis realised Paula was not going to let this just end with seeing what he looked like; she was already calling him 'our boy'. Dennis was going to object, but he had to stop himself, it was her boy, someone stealing him had not changed that fact, not in Paula's mind and therefore it should not be different in his mind either. "Dennis, are you listening?" Paula had noticed that Dennis had glassed over, a sure sign he was off track. "I was saying that the girls and I are going to Texas for a little holiday," she announced.

Dennis looked at Paula, "Whoa! What? Sorry, run that by me again?" he exclaimed. Paula knew this was going to be a hard sell, "The girls and I are going to see if we can get a look at him. I know you can't get out of your classes at the moment so we decided we would go without you and you can fly out for the weekend," Paula said, not leaving much space for Dennis to argue. Dennis realised it was pointless arguing with all three of them. Paula was hard enough, but add in two stubborn twins, and the case was hopeless. "Ok but what about the girl's school?" Dennis was clinging to the hope that reason would prevail. "The girls have done well this term, so I am sure a week or two away will be okay. They can do a project on the history of Texas while we are away." Paula grinned.

"Mum!" both girls protested. "Do we have to?" Gina asked. Steph elbowed her in the ribs, "Ok, I guess that would be okay." Gina replied. Dennis knew defeat when he saw it, "Great when do you all leave me in peace?" he asked, comically rubbing his head as though he had a splitting headache.

"Well," replied Paula, "we thought we should get on the road later today. The drive is about twelve hours and it would be good to get to Greenspan sometime later tomorrow." Dennis sighed, this was pointless, better to help them along rather than fight a clearly losing battle. "You're all packed aren't you?" Dennis asked the sheepish grins were all the answer he needed. "You know, I hate having no say in this family." He complained. "Dennis, darling, you do have a say, we just tell you what it is," said Paula getting out of her chair to give him a kiss. "Gross and Grosser," was Stephanie's only response while Gina was making dove noises. "Just you wait until you guys are in love," their mother threatened to smile, "just you wait."

Dennis managed to sneak out of class early in time to rush home and see his girls off on their ‘holiday'. All three had denied that his description of ‘stalking' was apter and insisted it was a ‘fact finding mission'. "Don't do anything stupid!" were his last words to Paula as she backed down the drive, a grin and a wave were all he got in reply. Dennis wandered back inside to get his keys. Sitting on the table was a picture the girls had printed out from the internet. It was a news article about a promising young runner by the name of James Kirkland, son of Texas's leading Gynaecological Surgeon, Simon Kirkland.

The drive to Greenspan was like most interstate drives, uneventful, punctuated with 7/11's for food, rest stops and gas stations to fill up the car. The night in the motel was clean but basic, as interstate ones often are. Paula and Dennis had brought the family to Texas a few years before but never to Greenspan. It looked a lot like any other Texan town. A wide main street with shops lining both sides of the road and plenty of parking. A central square shaped park sat where it should be adjacent to the town hall, and it all had the expected look of a small American town. To Paula it had that very American small town look like from the Back to the Future movie.

The concrete buildings and blacktop road were softened by the natural planting of trees currently without their leaves due to winter, such as it was down here in Texas. Overall it looked like a beautiful place to live. Paula pulled into a reasonable looking motel just off the main road, and she and the girls got out of the car and stretched. It was a pretty small car for a long journey, but Paula liked how fun it was to drive. "Right, let's see if they can put us up for the night," Paula said to Gina and Steph as they headed over to the motel office. "Mum, you're not Mary Mother of Jesus, and neither of us is Joseph. Don't embarrass us, just ask for a room." Gina begged.

Paula and the girls opened the door to the office and stepped in. "Howdy," came the distinctly Texan greeting from behind the counter, "how can I be helping you, ladies, today?" The woman behind the counter was probably in her late fifties and could have stood in for Dolly Parton in a pinch, both in looks and voice. The name on her name tag was Lexi.

"Hi, we are after a couple of rooms, one for me and one for my girls," Paula replied. "Oh now aren't you two like peas in a pod! How do you tell 'em apart? We got a couple of nice rooms looking out over the pool even if it is a bit cold for swimming', and there's even a door you can open between them both, and I'm sure we have it at just the right price for y'all. How does $45 a night sound?" Lexi pronounced all this in real Texan, and the price was an excellent deal. "That sounds great we will take them," Paula replied. "Oh that's just lovely," Lexi handed over the guest book for Paula to fill in their details, "and what brings you to Greenspan?" she asked. "Oh, just a holiday, a chance to get away with my girls," Paula replied. "That's just lovely," Lexi continued, "and where would you all be from?" Lexi's questions flowed thick and fast. "Oh us, we have come down from Denver, so not too far away," Paula replied truthfully. On the trip, they had decided it was much safer to keep to the truth as much as possible. Trying to get a fake story straight, and then keep it that way, was not something any of them thought they could manage.

The biggest part of the lie was the holiday part. They were here for only one reason, and that was to see James. "Just lovely" Lexi replied on learning where they were from. "Well, let's get the keys and get you'll settle in. Lexi turned and picked two sets of keys from a board behind the counter and directed Paula and the girls where to park. "You just park right out front of your rooms, did I mention they are quite lovely, our rooms?" Paula nodded. The key Paula thought was not to say too much or else they might be caught up in an hour long conversation with Lexi.

The rooms were nice, plain but nice, and the price was very reasonable. Lexi had even discounted the rate as they were going to stay for a couple of weeks and it was the off season. A connecting door was open between the two rooms, and Paula could hear the twins discussing some piece of man flesh that had been nosing around them over the last few weeks. "I bet if he asked you and you said no, he would ask me." Gina didn't think much of this one. "You're not giving him a chance." Steph countered. "Why give him a chance, we both know all he wants is to…"

Gina's speech trailed off as she realised Paula was in the other room. "Wants to do what, Stephanie?" Paula called out from the other room. "He wants to do Stephanie," Gina called out laughing. "Gina!" Paula was shocked, then realisation hit her hard, her girls were only one year of the age she was when she had the twins, oops she corrected herself, the triplets; this was going to take some getting use to. The twins were back to laughing at some private joke they had shared. Paula smiled, she loved it when they did that.

After dinner, Paula's phone rang. "Hey gorgeous, you get there safe and sound?" Dennis asked over the phone. "Hi, babe yes thanks, quite a drive but we got here in the end. Found this nice motel with a Dolly Parton look-a-like for you to gawk at when you arrive." Paula was grinning into the phone; she liked nothing better than giving Dennis a bit of stick. Like he would be interested. She thought to herself, confident in her man and their relationship. "Hey that sounds great, I think I have a lead for you on where you can find the boy," Dennis replied, not taking the Dolly Parton bait.

"Wow, that's quick work how did you find out that info?" Paula was getting excited. Gina and Steph had come into the room. "Hey, I'm putting you on speaker so you can tell us all." Paula switched the phone to the speaker. It was a trick the twins had taught her only the week before. Teenagers, Paula mused, really were better at this high tech stuff.

Dennis's voice came out clear over the speaker, "it was pretty simple really. After you had left I went back into the house and saw the news article about James the girls had printed out. Apparently, he is excellent at running, so I gave his school a quick call, and I posed as a reporter wanting to know when his next race is on. Well, it looks like there is an inter-school competition between Greenspan and some other school tomorrow at the Greenspan Athletic Park, and tomorrow just happens to the Founders Day holiday for Greenspan. Dennis advised. Paula could tell he was quite pleased with himself. "Hey, great work Sherlock," Gina called out. "Yay Dad, sneaky real sneaky," Steph chimed in.

Dennis felt pleased to have such high praise from his girls. Paula grinned at the girls, "Well, it looks like we have an outing planned for tomorrow, team. Great work honey," Paula switched the phone back off speaker and the girls returned to their room and switched on the television searching for a movie to watch. "I love you, Dennis." Paula said down the telephone, "I couldn't do this without you," she admitted. "Paula," Dennis's voice had softened, "this might not work, you know that right?" he said. Paula sighed, "I know honey, but I have to try, he's mine. I have to try right?" she asked. Dennis could hear the strain in Paula's voice, "I know darling, just stay safe, I miss you already." This comment brought a smile to Paula's face, "I love you two."

Both Dennis and Paula hung up; they had not often been apart in the ten years they had been married, and the separation was not something they particularly enjoyed. Paula could hear singing from the other room and immediately recognised the song Titanium from the movie Pitch Perfect. Oh well, that's always a good chick flick, bet the girls won't mind some company. She thought to herself.

She might just grab some chocolate and bust in on the girl's party. Hey, if they were lucky, she might even share.

12

Jan 22, 2013

James closed the door quietly not wanting to disturb his father. On race days he hated the distraction he brought. His father always wanted to add his ideas about how to run the race, and those ideas were almost always opposite to those of Coach Davidson. In one way James found this oddly comforting, knowing that if what his father said was in stark contrast to Coach then Coach was mostly likely right. James began walking towards Ash's house, intending to pick her up so they could walk together. Ash was sitting on the swing seat on the porch ready to go.

"So, you have a choice today." Ash proclaimed. "You may either sit here and swing with your best friend, 'or', and it is a big or, kick Lutridge Collage's arse." Ash was grinning. "Hmm, the swinging sounds pretty tempting, but I think I will go with the arse kicking." James smiled back. Ash was the perfect wingman; she always had his back, and James trusted her like no one else. She would not be offering technique tips or strategies to win the race. No, Ash would just be there cheering him on, win, loose or something else altogether.

Ash would be a rock he could rely on. Their relationship was something he had given thought to of late, but he was not sure how Ash felt. James knew how he felt and those feelings could probably stuff up a great friendship. Ash started walking. "So did the mighty Dr Kirkland offer any pearls of running wisdom today?" she asked as they walked towards the school. James laughed, "Nope, I managed to slip out before receiving the excellent running knowledge," he replied. "Sneaky, I like it. But I doubt your sneakiness will get you out of the Jones' speech," stated Ash. "Oh great, way to go Ash just ruin my pre-race mental prep." James laughed. "It's ok James, you didn't need any prep, you're already mental," Ash replied, punching him in the arm.

This was just what James needed the mindless banter of two good friends. What he didn't need was the Jones speech. James had got into the habit of changing into his running gear early. 'the Jones' had an annoying habit of barging into the changing room to give a speech about how James was representing more than himself and his family name, how his performance reflected on the school and he MUST do his utmost to run fast, very fast and win.

It was not the most inspiring speech and even less so when you are still standing in your boxer shorts half dressed for your race. Today he had beaten the Jones by a good five minutes, so he was fully dressed for the Jones' prep talk speech. It was just like normal with all the same words, and like usual, meant nothing to James. His mind was already in the race, he knew he had trained well and that he was probably as fast as he could be, so today win or lose he would give it his best.

Ash was not much of a sporty girl. It was strange, to her mind, and to many others, that she hung out with a jock. But James was not a traditional kind of Jock. He was excellent at sport, but he was also pretty good at almost anything he tried. Math came easy, so did English, History, and Science. About the only thing that James sucked at was art. James couldn't draw to save himself. Ash had at one time loaned him her camera, but most of his shots were blurry or the subject way out of frame. The differences between them might have been vast but firm friends they were.

Ash took her usual seat up the top of the stands, away from what she called 'James Groupie Girls' who seemed to hover near the finish line. They all appeared to want to be the first to congratulate him if he won or lost. That sort of girly behaviour made Ash sick. Why they couldn't just like James for who he was not how he performed. Ash shook her head. Ash looked at the stand at all the people there.

This was Greenspan home turf so most of the people she could name, it was not like Greenspan was a big town. Ash could even recognise some of the visitors. They all bunched together near the bottom of the stand to cheer on their runners as they passed by. Ash was suddenly drawn to three girls sitting in the middle of the stand. They, Ash did not know, and somehow they just didn't fit the mould. What was it about them? Ash asked herself. Perhaps a look from the front would help. Ash got up and made her way down the stands and once at the bottom headed over to the drink vending machine. Popping in some loose change, she took her time selecting a drink while out of the corner of her eye gave them the once over.

"Damn, they all look the same." Ash mused to herself. Ash cracked open a Pepsi and made her way back up the stands. This time she took the centre aisle steps so she could get a better look. As she climbed the steps Ash got a much better look at the three girls, no, one was not a girl but a woman, but the other two, it was like seeing double. They so have to be twins, Ash thought to herself, but the older one, perhaps a sister?

The another thing that caught Ash's attention was the SLR camera with a gigantic lens. Ash admired the camera and lens combo as she walked past, "Hey, nice kit." Ash said to the twin girl holding the camera. Gina looked up at the goth looking girl walking past. "Oh, yeah, thanks," she said, looking a bit embarrassed. Ash paused, "Canon 7D?" Gina glanced down at the camera, "Yes, you know your gear." Gina replied. Ash paused her climb, "I'm more of a Nikon girl myself, but Canon's ok. Well, later." Ash moved on. Weird, she thought to herself. The three of them didn't fit in somehow. What she was certain about was that they were all related, I mean the twins were obviously related, but the older woman must have been their mother. I hope I look that good if I ever have teenagers. Ash thought to herself. Like I will ever mate and have kids. Climbing the stairs back up she decided she would move seats just to keep a closer eye on these three.

13

The cheerleaders from both schools entered the field to the cheering of the crowd. Each performed their respective routines. As far as Ash was concerned, cheerleading was not a sport; it was something parents made their girls do to keep them off drugs. Ash, unlike the crowd, had no interest in a bunch of girls being, well a bunch of girls, so she continued to watch the three newcomers. They, unlike the rest of the visitors, didn't cheer when either school's cheer team performed, rather they just clapped politely at the end of each display. The cheerleading show had ended, and now a cheer went up from the home crowd as James ran out onto the track.

Ash noticed the twin with the camera swing it up quickly and run off maybe a dozen shots. Ash could hear the distinctive 7D shutter sound from where she was sitting. Damn, those Canons can shoot fast. Ash couldn't remember how many shots per second, but she did know it was at least twice what her ageing Nikon could manage.

The home crowd continued to cheer as three of their other runners took to the field and made their way to their starting positions. Ash noticed the Canon had gone silent and the girl was not taking any shots of the other Greenspan or Ludridge athletes. As the visitors running starting coming out Ash expected to see the camera back in use, but it stayed lowered. Ash looked around the stand and noticed a man in a police uniform standing at the base of the stands looking slightly confused. When he spotted Ash, he began to make his way up to where she was seated. His path took him directly past the three newcomers. "Hello," he said as he climbed the steps past. "Oh, hello officer," Paula replied.

The police officer continued past them and on reaching Ash sat down. "You sick or something, Ash?" Officer Ben Smith asked opening a packed lunch. "Nope, why do you ask Officer Smith, have I done something wrong?" Ash asked laughing. "Not really, I just ask as I have never seen you sit over here in the stands. What gives, is there some boy I need to have a little talk to?" Ben asked. "You, and I, wish," Ash replied while stealing a cookie from her father's lunch and looking at James. "That's stealing you know!" Ben stated.

Ash made a show of putting her wrists together, "Arrest me, Officer, I did it, take me away." They both laughed. "So is fast feet going to bring it home for Greenspan today?" Ben asked, referring to James. "I think he will, he's got the skill, and he snuck out before the father speech, so I give him 7:1 odds," Ash stated. Ben looked at his daughter, "Hey, you got some illegal betting ring running I should know about?" "Why? You want in?" she joked, as she pretended to offer him odds. They both laughed again. Ash loved her dad. He was always very laid back and would often make time during his week to attend school events like this just to get more time with her, but he never made it a big deal. Ash slipped her arm around him and gave him a hug.

Paula had watched the Police officer climb the steps with mounting dread. We are not doing anything wrong; she kept telling herself over and over. Her heart nearly jumped out of her chest when he said hello. The girls turned to watch him climb to where the Nikon girl was sitting behind them with a sense of relief; he wasn't here for them. Silly! Thought Paula to herself, as they had not committed any crime. In fact, the reverse was the case - they were trying to solve a crime. Paula glanced over her shoulder to see the Nikon girl put her arm around the office and give him a hug. She must be his daughter, Paula realised. Their position half way up the stands was a double edged sword. It provided a fantastic angle for Gina's long zoom lens to photograph James, but it left Paula too far away for her to have a real look at her son. Gina leant over to show Paula a few of the photos.

James is gorgeous, Paula realised. It was no wonder there were a bunch of girls hollering and cheering him on, his straight blond hair was just slightly too long, giving him a 'who cares' sort of attitude, and with his physical, athletic build, he exuded a male confidence that was appealing. James wore a tight yellow athletic singlet and black running shorts. On his feet were a pair of day-glow orange Nike running shoes.

"He's a hunk," Steph commented. "Steph, he's our brother!" Gina hissed under her breath. "Just saying, he's a looker. Wow, our brother's a real looker." Steph replied. Paula sighed, he was such a good-looking young man perhaps his life was better, after all, having been taken from her. Paula look around the stands searching for any sign of Dr Kirkland but finding none. I wonder if Mrs Kirkland is here, Paula thought to herself. Gina was thinking the same, "Do you believe that we will see his Mother or

Father?" she asked. "Not sure, we might have to wait until the end and see who he leaves with," Paula replied.

James turned and searched the stands for Ash. She was not in her usual spot and it took him a moment to place her and her father. James gave them a quick wave and a thumbs up. His eyes drifted down to three women sitting a bit below Ash and her dad. A weird feeling of Déjà vu like he had seen them before. The hairs on his arms were standing up. That's crazy he thought to himself, it is just pre-race nerves. Shaking his head he moved off to the starting blocks.

Paula and the girls froze as James seemed to wave at them and then give them a thumbs up. Paula suddenly realised it was not for them but the police officer and his daughter sitting up behind them. That's interesting; Paula thought he has completely ignored all the adoring girls at the start finish line. Perhaps the girl above was his girlfriend.

The news article the girls had found mentioned that James was a middle distance runner. The announcer had said this was an 800m race, and it seemed clear that James was the favourite. The runners all took to the starting blocks and suddenly the gun went off for a start. All nine runners started cleanly, quickly settling into their rhythm. James was three back from the leader, and he seemed to be content to keep to this position.

By halfway round the first lap, the runners had formed an almost single line. The three girls could clearly see James's yellow singlet and orange shoes. As the runners came past for their first lap, the visiting crowd exploded in cheers as it was clear that ahead of James were two of their own. As the first runners crossed the halfway point it was clear that the front three had broken off from the pack. James was taking a slightly wider line as he prepared for his attack. Paula marvelled at his form as flew past the stands. Over her shoulder Paula could hear the goth girl saying "Wait for it, here comes the flying feet move, Go, James, Go!"

There was no way James could have made out the call from Ash in the stands above, but at that very moment he seemed to change gear and drew from some extra energy reserves the front runners could not seem to tap into. Slipping out into the next lane, James's speed leapt, and he charged past the two runners on the outside. But James was not content to just get in front, and his pace did not slow. Gina watched the faces of the two runners he had passed in the viewfinder of her camera and could see they knew that they had just been beaten. James charged into the home straight heading for the finish.

"Something's wrong" Gina was the first to feel it. "It's his left leg or, I don't know, yes, it's his left leg." Steph was visibly rubbing her left leg as she felt James pain. "I don't see anything," Paula exclaimed. "Are you sure?" Paula's question hung in the air as suddenly James pulled up short. He glanced over his shoulder and seeing the next two runners were coming hard he dug in and bravely tried to push through the pain.

His left leg was not holding his weight correctly, and his only option was to half run, half limp, towards the finish. With every second James came closer to the finish line but the runners behind closed the gap rapidly. As James came within the final meters of the finish, he could hear the sounds of the two runners behind him. James threw himself at the line knowing this was going to hurt, but the stinging of the track surface was far worse than he thought. It was like his skin was being pulled down a cheese grater and he screamed out in pain.

14

The marshals rushed over to James and reached him moments before Coach Davidson. Coach looked at James, "James, are you ok?" The absurdity of his comment was not lost on him. There were grazes all the way down James' left leg and lower arm. "I'm Ok," James managed to say, "I think it was my hamstring. I don't think I can walk properly. Did I win?" James grinned through the pain. Coach Davidson shook his head, "You crazy bastard, yes but only just." James was the only person that Coach Davidson would speak to this way. Helping James to his feet, they turned to face the stands as a cheer erupted from the home team. James gave them all a big smile and wave and with Coach's help limped off the track.

"Damn, that hurts," Gina commented. "You two ok?" Paula asked. The twins were rubbing their left legs and were in obvious pain. "That was weird; the pain was much worse than before. Do you think it was just as painful for James? Cause that hurt." Gina asked. "Maybe we felt it more because we are closer?" Steph replied. They all stopped talking as Ash, and her father came down from their seats above.

Ash was feeling weird; her gaze had shifted to the twins as they started to feel James' pain yet James was still running strong. It was like watching a mirror as both girls winced with pain and started rubbing their left legs. They were in pain; the mother was apparently talking to them about it, and there was concern on her face, then for some strange reason they all looked at James. Ash had followed their gaze and moments later you could see James was in trouble. As Ash and her father walked past the three newcomers, Ben gave them a friendly wave and said: "See you later folks." Ash locked eyes with the twins and gave them a strange look; she was tempted to stop and ask what was wrong, but she was keen to check up on James. When Ben and Ash reached the bottom of the stand, she glanced up to see the twins hobbling down the steps. The mother was now holding the camera helping the girl with the camera and her sister, as they descended. Something is not right here. Ash thought, but she could not put her finger on it. She hoped she would get to the bottom of it, but right now she needed to go and see James.

James sat propped up on a stretcher just outside the ambulance. The paramedic had applied a dressing to his arm and leg, and other than that he looked fine. Ash pushed through the crowd of onlookers and went straight up to James. "How's the patient?" Ash directed her question to the paramedic. "You family?" he asked. "I'm his wife, Cupcake. Now how is he?" Ash replied, lying. The paramedic gave Ash his very best 'Pull the other one' look. "I'm fine, and I can answer for myself, thanks," James replied sensing Ash was about to make a rather large scene. "A few grazes and they want to X-ray my leg. Coach thinks it's my hamstring. You want to bum a ride in the blood bus?" James asked Ash. The paramedic looked over at James, "I'm sorry sir but only family in the ambulance."

At that moment Ben arrived and saw Ash was on her way to going ballistic managed to intercede. "Hey Stan," Ben said holding his hand out. "Oh hi Ben, how's it going?" replied the paramedic, shaking Ben's offered hand. "Good, hey you think you could make an exception this once? James and my daughter here are like brother and sister." Ben let the question hang in the air. The paramedic looked uncertain but then changed his mind. "Ok, but just this once," he replied. Turning to face Ash he grinned, "One wrong move Miss, and I will kick you out even if the ambulance is still running." Ash smiled. "I like you," she said, patting Stan on the cheek. "Come on champ, let's go see if you have a brain." Ash climbed into the ambulance while Stan and Ben helped load James. "Your, daughter huh?" Stan asked. "Yup" replied Ben grinning. "Quite a firecracker," Stan said closing the doors. "Yup, you're not wrong there. Later Stan" Ben waved as Stan got in the driver's seat to leave.

Paula had got the girls to hold back as she quietly slipped through the crowd to the front. There, not more than two meters away, sat her son. The goth looking girl was there and climbed into the ambulance as the paramedic and the cop they had seen earlier loaded James in. He was all she had ever imagined and more. He had a strong face and an easy smile. His blond hair was just a tad too long for the mother in her, but no doubt teenage girls loved it. Tears started to run down her cheek. Paula felt a hand on her shoulder and turned to see Steph standing there behind her. Steph guided her back through the crowd to where Gina was waiting. "Mum, this is never going to work if you get this emotional" Gina stated. Paula nodded. "I know, I just had to get a closer look. Isn't he beautiful?" Paula asked. Gina nodded.

The three of them walked back to the car. "The holiday angle is going to wear pretty thin the longer we stay." Steph pointed out. "I mean we can't just wander around his school saying we are on holiday, now can we? And that is the only place we will ever see him now." Paula and the girls got back in the car. Paula paused, "You're right Steph, you can't wonder around the school while on holiday." Paula said. Paula glanced back in the rearview mirror at the twins. Gina looked straight back at her mother, "Oh, no, you do not think what I think you're thinking are you?" "Mum, that's crazy," Steph said catching on suddenly. "Ok, tell me why it's so crazy? Paula demanded. Gina took a breath, "It's mad because you want us to switch schools and go where James goes so that we can get close." Gina replied, getting it right first time. "What, you think you're not up to it?" Paula liked baiting the girls almost as much as when she did it to Dennis. "When you think about it, this may be the only way we can get through to James and we are going to need some evidence that he is even your brother." Paula pointed out.

There was silence in the car as both twins digested what Paula had said. Steph was the first to break the silence, "We are going to need a good reason for moving here," she pointed out. "Is that a yes?" Paula was getting excited. "This is nuts, but ok I'm in," Gina said. "I guess I'm in two," Steph added. "Man is Dad going to flip," Gina declared. That comment broke the tension in the car, and they all burst out laughing. Paula put the car into gear and reversed out of the park. "Ok, back to the motel. We need to get our story straight before meeting your new Principal tomorrow," Paula stated, "Oh and there is the little issue of how we break this to your Dad."

As James expected it was a pulled hamstring. The pain of the injury was the least of his concerns. The Dr. had advised that it was a grade two tear and he should make a full recovery in about six to eight weeks. Coach Davidson sighed a sigh of relief that suddenly evaporated when Dr Kirkland came barging through the door. "Oh no," was all Ash managed under her breath as he entered. Dr. Kirkland was ropable, "What the hell happened, Davidson?" he demanded. "Dad, it's just a hamstring, I'm fine!" James said, coming to the defence of his coach. "Be quiet James! I am speaking to Mr Davidson." Dr Kirkland shot back at James. "If there is any permanent damage I will sue you till the cows come home, I will make sure you never teach another student ever again." Coach Davidson stood quietly and took the verbal abuse hurled by Dr Kirkland.

Right at this point the surgeon entered having heard Kirkland's outburst from out in the hallway. "Simon, how are you?" Dr Cole asked. "I see you have seen our champion and that he is doing very well. Even managed to finish the race I hear." Dr Cole continued not wanting for Dr Kirkland to answer or get a word in edgeways. "I am happy to say that the tear was only just a grade two, James should be back up and running in no time. As I am sure you are aware grade two's take about six to eight weeks to come right and I, expect a full recovery." Dr Cole did not like how Kirkland pushed his son or what he had heard Kirkland saying to the coach. "Right then I think it would be a good time for us to leave James to his recovery. When you feel ready to move, James just press the nurse call bell, and we will help you to head home."

With the doctor's orders, they all filed out of the room. Ash had slipped into the bathroom as Dr Kirkland had barged in. She now peeked out, making sure the coast was clear. "All clear then," she said, climbing onto the end of James' bed. "You not leaving yet then?" James asked, quite pleased Ash was hanging around. "Well from what I can see on this chart they have not tested to see if you have a brain, best if I wait to see if you do," Ash said while looking at the chart. "Hey did you know you are AB- blood type?" Ash asked. "No, so what?" James replied. "Well, it's like one of the rarest types out there. I'm surprised they haven't stuck you with a needle and drained some out for other people." Ash joked. James shifted on the bed to get more comfortable. "You are a nerd Ash. I mean, who knows that stuff?" Ash grinned at James, "So your Dad took it well," she remarked. "Whatever, just you wait until I get home, all hell will break loose," James replied. "That is the type of outburst one does not do in public."

Dr Cole knocked and came back into the room. "Ok James, I think we can send you home as there is no need to keep you overnight. I have prescribed some pain relief, and you should be ok to go back to school tomorrow if you feel up to it. Now would you like a wheelchair or do you think you can manage on crutches?" Dr Cole asked. "Wheelchair, totally the wheelchair!" Ash exclaimed. "I will push you anywhere," said Ash laughing. "Crutches will be all right, thanks, Dr Cole, oh and by the way, I think this girl has escaped from the mental ward," James replied earning him a slap from Ash. "No problem, and well done today, perhaps take it a little easier next time, alright?" Dr Cole exited the room to get James some crutches.

On arriving home, James was surprised to find his father was not that angry at all. Several reporters had already been in contact, hoping to get a photo and a story of the boy who didn't give up. It would seem that his father quite enjoyed the attention James had earned the family name. James could only wonder what he would have said if he had not managed to win. Closing the door to his bedroom he went and sat at his desk. The familiar feeling of loneliness came over him.

It was times like this that James felt the loss of his mother the most. Olivia Kirkland was a tough nut, but she was always very loving. James could still remember the feeling of being wanted by his mum. Until she died, he had been unaware of his father's indifference towards him. Now it was like they were two strangers living under the same roof. Dr Kirkland provided the basics that James needed, food, shelter, money, and the best schooling. He provided everything, everything except the one thing James truly needed, love. Well at least he had Ash, even if it was only as a friend, she was the closest thing he had to a loving family.

15

Ash strode into the police gun range as if she owned the place. In truth she had been coming here since she was eight, so no one questioned her as she pressed in a set of ear plugs and settled her safety glasses in place. She quietly moved up towards her father as he stood to shoot, making sure she was just within his peripheral vision so as not to startle him. "Hey Ash," her father shouted. Ben continued shooting his card. His stance was relaxed and as Ash watched the monitor overhead she saw Ben's last five rounds carve a nice ragged circle in the centre of the bull.

The slide on the pistol locked back in the open position, an indication it was empty. Ben ejected the magazine, working the action a few more times, to ensure the weapon was safe. His final inspection was to check the chamber one last time. Finding everything as it should be, Ben placed the pistol on the bench and removed his ear protectors. Ash did the same. "So, how's Fast Feet?" Ben asked. "Surviving. The hospital was all right, but I doubt home will be as easy. Did his hamstring," Ash replied.

"You looked pissed," was Ben's reply "Want to shoot a steel round to take your mind off it?" he asked. "Sounds great. You gonna see if you can take me?" Ash challenged, knowing her Dad would not even try. Ash wondered over to her father's gun case sitting on the table against the back wall. She selected her personal favourite, a beautiful jet black H & K P30 with a speed holster. Ash liked this particular gun as it was a bit smaller than most of her father's personal weapons and it fitted her hand better. Ben came over and helped load four clips.

Ben and some of the other officers had set up a steel shooting range outside. It gave them the chance to improve their reaction times and engage in some friendly competition. Ash stood ready at the outside range starting position. Her hands were by her side, and the P30 was nestled in its holster. Ash forced her breathing into a slow and regular pattern.

Her father held the starter up behind her head and depressed the button causing it to beep. Ben marvelled at the fluid speed of his daughter's draw, as Ash's hand came down to the pistol and smoothly removed it from the holster. The P30 was immediately becoming an extension of her arms. In no time the sounds of rounds hitting steel were echoing around the range. Ash moved to her next position dropping five more targets. Turning ninety degrees right she acquired stage three and the next five and put them down in quick succession. As Ash ran to the fourth stage, she cleanly ejected the empty magazine and with her left hand slid the next full one home.

Ben watched as a small group of police officers gathered to view Ash in action. It had been more than a few years since any of these men or women had been able to outscore Ben's daughter. The sound of shooting stopped, and Ben automatically stopped the clock, "Damn, three minutes, ten seconds." he announced as a cheer went up from those watching. Ash holstered her P30 and came over. "So how'd I do?" She asked. "Hmm, ok, I guess. Your mag changes could have been a bit smoother," Ben replied. Ash tilted her head, a mannerism her mother used to use, "Don't mess with me, I have a gun. What was my time?" Ash threatened. "Three, ten," Ben replied holding his hands up in mock surrender, grinning. "Wow, five seconds less and I'm an international grade," Ash pointed out. Ben put his arm around his daughter as they walked back inside. "Just remember, fast is slow but smooth is fast," Ben said repeating the speed shooters' mantra. Several officers high five her as she and Ben walked back inside. The time spent target shooting had dampened Ash's annoyance at how James was treated. Some people treat their dogs better than Dr Kirkland treated James, she thought. At least her Dad respected her.

16

That night Paula called Dennis to give him an update. "You would not believe it, the girls were in agony, and they seemed to sense it would happen before you could see it," Paula said, recounting the event. "Dennis I need you to send me the girls academic records, birth certificates and passports," Paula stated. Dennis began sensing something himself, "What do you need those for?" he asked. "I'm going to enrol the girls in James' school," Paula replied. Dennis inwardly groaned, "Paula, is that wise?"

Dennis was massaging his temples, just trying to keep up with Paula was giving him a headache. "What other option do we have? We can't make a direct approach to James as he would never believe us, and if we show our hand to Dr Kirkland he may go to ground, and we will lose him." Dennis had to agree with Paula. She was right - they would have to see how this would unfold, and playing tourist would only wash for so long before people started asking questions. "Ok, but you can't give the school the girls' birth certificates, they have your maiden name on them! Best if you just stick with the passports, they're in Farley, not Johnson," Dennis pointed out. Paula smacked her hand into her forehead. "That was close, I would have just given the school the birth certificates and if Dr Kirkland had ever checked…" Paula left the potential outcome hanging as they both knew what it could mean.

"Alright then, I will courier the girls' stuff to you tomorrow. What are you going to say about your work?" Dennis asked. Paula had thought this part through, "I am going to tell them I am looking at setting up a restoration business here in Greenspan. It might mean I have to go and see some items in people's homes, and I might be able to get them to talk at the same time. I could even scour the local second-hand shops for some new stock," Paula explained.

Dennis knew a lost cause when he saw one, fighting Paula would not end well. It was better all-around if he just helped her any way he could. "Ok, that sounds reasonable. I better go and find all those files, so you get them before the weekend. Love you lots." Dennis hung up. Wow, this is moving fast! He thought to himself, but Paula seemed to have it under control, other than the birth certificate thing. He would just have to trust her and the girls and do whatever he could to help, they were, after all, a team. Dennis opened his diary and took a look at the next couple of weeks. Drat, booked solid, he thought to himself, seeing the number of classes blocking out each day. Guess it will be a couple of weeks before I can join the girls.

17

Jan 23, 2013

Paula called the school early to organise a meeting with the Principal so they could enrol Gina and Stephanie. The earliest appointment they could get was just after lunch. The school looked like most other public schools. In this case, it was made from a yellow-colored brick and looked very well maintained. Students hung around outside despite the temperature being in the low 40's, clustered in small groups with similar interests. All the natural groupings seemed to be in evidence. There were the cool kids with the latest fashions, the jocks, the free spirits, and pretty much everything in-between. Paula and the girls made their way to the office to meet with the Principal named Mrs Jones. The walk to the principal's office told them a lot about the school and its principal. Paula had seen hospitals with less shiny floors. Lining the walls were cabinets filled with trophies and pictures of past and current athletes.

After a fifteen-minute wait at reception Paula and the girls were shown through to the principal's office. Paula could tell she would not like Mrs Jones the moment they shook hands. There seemed to be a nasty streak to her that was hard to pin down, but Paula often relied on her gut reaction, and her response to Mrs Jones was not a good one. She was going to have to suck it in and deal with it if they were going to pull this off.

"So Mrs Farley, how may we help you?" Mrs Jones asked, sitting back down behind a massive oak desk.

"Well, I would like to enrol my twin girls into your school, if I may," Replied Paula, using her best manners.

"I see," replied Mrs Jones, "Hmm, we are quite a popular school, you know so the only thing I could offer is to put them in the same class. I hope that is not an inconvenience," Jones replied, not caring if it were an inconvenience at all.

"No, that will be quite acceptable, that way they will at least know each other," Paula pointed out. "Yes, yes, well that is one of the reasons I suggested it," Mrs Jones replied. "And may I enquire as to your reasons for choosing Greenspan High Mrs Farley? I believe I saw you and your daughters at the race yesterday?" Paula had to dig in to regain her composure. Had they stood out that much? She wondered to herself.

Gina decided to answer, "We had researched your school on the internet and we liked what we saw academically, we thought that seeing Greenspan on the sporting field would help us to make our decision. We were most impressed with the guy who fell over; he just kept going even though he was injured." Gina could lie just as well as Mrs Jones.

Mrs Jones puffed up enjoying the compliment, "Yes, well not all our athletes are the same calibre as James Kirkland, but I think you will find our physical education department top notch. In fact, I intend to place your girls in the very same class as James," explained Mrs Jones to Paula. Gina and Steph knew they had to hide their excitement. They took strength knowing that they were both fighting the urge to grin and high-five. Paula looked over at them and marvelled at their poker faces.

It was more than any of them had hoped for. Not only were they in the same school but placed in the very class with James. "And may I ask what you do Mrs Farley?" Mrs Jones casually enquired. "Oh, it's Miss Farley," Paula lied, "I work with antiques, restoring them for sale or private collectors. I am hoping to generate enough business here to set up shop in Texas; I am not much of a city girl, so Greenspan looked like the perfect spot, close enough but not too close to Texas," Paula replied.

Mrs Jones seemed to like this answer. "Well I think you will find many monied families here in Greenspan who would use your services Miss Farley, I wish you luck," Mrs Jones rose from her desk. "Well, I guess that all we require now is some details about you and your girls and we can get things moving. If you would come with me, I will introduce you to our admissions clerk, and she will take down your details."

Paula filled out the numerous application forms while the girls sat waiting. Paula turned to look at the sound of the door behind them opening as Mrs Jones walked in followed by the goth girl from the day before. "Mrs Farley, um, Girls," Mrs Jones was going to try to remember which was which of the twins but decided to give up, they looked too similar for her to be sure. "This is one of the students in the girls class, Ashlie. She will help orientate you girls, when you start school tomorrow. I will leave you to get to know one another." Mrs Jones left the room and closed the door.

Ash stood staring at the twins. "Hey, I'm Gina," Gina said by way of greeting. "And I'm Stephanie, but everyone calls me Steph," Steph added. Ash nodded, "Hi, you were at the race yesterday." Ash replied with a statement rather than a question.

The admissions clerk flagged Paula back over, "Excuse me, Miss Farley, I think you have missed a question, what are the girls' blood types?" she asked.

"Oh, sorry, how did I miss that field. They are both AB-. Twins, you see." Paula explained. Ash looked at Paula and then back at the twins. This place seemed to be teaming with rare blood types these days! She thought. Ash had planned to ditch these two 'goodie two shoes' kids as soon as possible, but there was that funny feeling again, Yes, something was going on here, she might just need to keep these two within sight, she told herself.

18

Jan 24, 2013

Ash wasn't waiting for James to walk with to school, his father had insisted on driving him. There was no thought in Dr Kirkland's head of asking if Ash wanted a ride to school with James. Truth be told, Dr Kirkland was only doing it as it made him look like a loving father. No doubt he would make sure that as many people saw him drop James off as possible. The snub didn't bother Ash least of all. She wanted to be a little bit early to intercept the two new girls anyway.

This would be the first time Ash had followed 'the Jones' instructions to the letter. This was only because Ash's desires did not run contrary to 'the Jones's'. Ash arrived at school and chose a good spot to wait and watch. She sensed there was something more to the Farley girls and their mother, but at this point, nothing was making any sense. She planned on finding out what it was by spending as much time with the Farley twins as possible. With James off his feet, it gave her just a bit more time to dedicate to solving this mystery.

Paula pulled into the school parking lot. They were early. The twins and Dennis liked to joke that Paula was chronically early and never late, and today was no exception. "Way to go, Mom, the first day of school and now we are the nerdy early kids," joked Gina.

Paula ignored the comment, "Remember to keep to the truth as much as possible… within reason," Paula reminded them. "And have fun with your brother," she added, smiling sadly.

Ash watched as the little red hot hatch pulled in. She didn't follow cars, so to her, it was simply red and sporty looking. If she were honest with herself, it was the kind of car she would buy, if she ever had money for a car. Gina and Steph hopped out and started over towards the school. Ash stood up and moved to intercept them. "Hey," Ash said moving up alongside them.

"Hi," both twins replied in unison.

"So you're Gina, and you're Steph right?" Ash asked.

Gina and Steph stopped and looked at Ash. "Wow, how did you get that? Luck, or have you figured it out?" Gina asked, apparently surprised.

"Almost no one can tell us apart," Steph added.

Ash grinned, "I wasn't 100% sure but I think you both have slightly different mannerisms, and I tend to notice things that other people don't." Ash left the accusation hang in the air. Neither Gina or Steph seemed to show any reaction to her comment. Ash broke the silence, "So I guess I should show you around," she said, leading the way towards the entrance.

One of the advantages of being a twin is you can almost always tell what your twin was thinking. Right at this moment Gina and Steph both knew Ash was fishing, but they were unsure of what. Gina was desperate for a chance to speak to Steph alone. Steph looked over at Gina; the message was clear, 'I got that hint two, stick close.' The school was much like the one they had left at home. Long corridors lined with lockers. They were each issued one and given a combination lock. Classrooms came off the main corridors just like their school at home. Other than the different colour bricks, (their old school had red ones) this could have been a more flashy version of their old school.

Being a more traditional school their whole class moved about the school together, attending the same topics in different rooms. For most of the classes, the twins were seated at the back of the class in whatever spare desks there were. The science class, however, was different. The teacher decided that he would split up Ash and James and then pair them with Gina and Steph. This worked out well as James could not move around the room very well on his crutches, so the teacher moved him to the front of the room with Gina, and Steph moved back to pair with Ash.

Gina could not be more delighted; she would now be closer to James than ever. Ash was less than impressed to look up and see James and Gina laughing when something went wrong with a chemistry experiment. She wondered if her feelings were jealousy, James was her friend and it felt bad that he had quickly bonded with Gina. Ash shook her head. As far as James knew, she and James were just friends, and he could see whomever he wanted. That didn't mean that it didn't hurt. Gina and James connected almost immediately. Gina was pleased to learn that James was not just a 'jock' but incredibly intelligent and hard working. He commanded the respect of the other students by his actions. Gina had to admit that if she had not been his sister she would have been attracted to him. Feeling the unspoken question, Gina turned to face Steph. Gina knew that look; Steph wanted to swap places.

Standing in the toilets Gina and Steph debated the pros and cons. "You know this could go bad, Steph?" Gina exclaimed.

"So why have you started to swap clothes then?" Steph countered, while also changing out of her top.

Gina sighed, "Because, nut case, arguing with you is like banging my head into a wall!" she replied.

Steph grinned, "Off with your kit then."

This was the risky part of any swap. Having spent time with Ash and James, there would have been conversations that the other did not know about. As usual, they did their best to bring each other up to speed on the topics and any important points that might give the game away. Gina was right, there was a significant risk, but they were experts in pulling this off back in Denver where people knew them better. Greenspan should be a walk in the park. Gina and Steph headed off to the cafeteria to get lunch. Picking a table on their own, they were both surprised when Ash came over and sat down with them. Ash looked at each of them; something was different, she thought to herself. Suddenly she realised what it was. They have swapped clothes; they are swapping places. Ash decided not to let them know she had figured it out; no she would not show her hand just yet.

James cruised over on his crutches making it look easy like he did with almost everything. "Hey," he said to no one in particular, "mind if I join you?" James plonked himself down, not waiting for an answer. "So what do you two do for fun?" he asked Gina and Steph. Gina looked over at Steph, and she got the message. "Gina's into photography, totally mad on it. Give her some time, and she will have you modelling for her." Gina replied, making out she was Steph.

Steph nodded, she knew how to play the game, "Begged Mom to get me a pretty decent Canon camera a few years ago. Now I have to ask her to buy me new gear like lenses and stuff." Steph replied. Ash watched with amazement as Steph pretended to be Gina.

"And what about you?" James asked Gina, who he thought was Steph.

"Totally into music." Gina declared.

"Like who?" Ash asked seeing if she could catch them out.

"Oh pretty much anything," Gina replied, "have you heard of Ok Go, Mumford and Sons or Walk off the Earth?" she asked.

Ash nodded, "My personal fave is Walk off the Earth," she declared.

Steph shook her head in wonder, "Wow I thought my sister was the only one who listened to that junk, who knew."

Ash decided to see if she could trip them up by changing direction dramatically. "So what's it like being a twin, do you guys ever swap places for fun?" she asked innocently. Gina and Steph didn't lose a beat.

"We use to do it all the time. We started doing it to mum when we were little. Then at school…"

Steph cut in, "when we had a math test, I would switch with Gina, cause she couldn't add for nuts." she finished laughing.

Gina continued, "Mom got real good at catching us out, and now we would get grounded forever if we tried it." she added looking at Ash. Steph glanced over at Gina, and both girls knew Ash had been fishing.

James laughed, "Well it must be fun having a sister, Ash and I are both only children. I guess that's why we are so close." he added. Ash nodded, "Well someone has to keep an eye on the cripple here." she replied pointing at James.

That night back at the motel Gina and Steph discussed what had happened at school. "She's fishing." Steph declared. "Yes but what for?" Gina added, "I am pretty sure she knew we had swapped places. She even asked if we ever traded places, like she was trying to catch us out." "I am confident no one heard us change in the bathroom, do you think she can tell us apart?" Steph asked. "She did guess earlier in the day; I think she is watching us." Gina let the statement sink in. "Well, no matter what she knows, or what she thinks she knows, we are going to have to be very careful," Gina replied.

19

The twins were an instant hit at school, and all the cool kids tried to pull them into their social circle. They certainly would have fit in with them. They dressed well, were good looking but also very approachable. Strangely they seemed to prefer hanging out with Ash and James. The four continued to meet at lunch. Gina and Steph had decided that switching places were now too risky with Ash snooping around. Keeping both James and Ash close seemed to be the safest option at present.

Ash and Gina had taken to taking photos with one another. It became a bit of a contest to see who could get the best photo. One Saturday the four of them went out to the park to take pictures. The four of them naturally got on well. Gina and Ash's shared interest in photography had them trying out each other's area of interest. Gina loved taking photos of people and sports, whereas Ash liked nature and landscapes. Ash watched as Gina used a large Sigma lens to zoom in on a couple sitting on a park bench in the distance. "You prefer they don't see you, huh?" she asked.

Gina nodded while looking through the viewfinder. "I like to capture people candidly. It seems more natural that way. If you ask to take their picture, they put on a fake look. You know, that fake smile people have, when they know they are having their photo taken?" she replied.

Ash nodded, she knew that well. "That's why I stick to nature; no one fakes you out there. And the another thing is the lenses are cheaper," she replied laughing.

Gina grinned at Ash, "Yea, well that 28mm f1.8, you have there can't have been cheap." she said gesturing towards the lens attached to the Nikon hanging around Ash's neck.

Ash took her camera from around her neck, "You want to have a play?" offering Gina her Nikon.

Gina nodded, "Swap you." she replied handing Ash the Canon with the large zoom lens.

James and Steph sat on the grass in the shade under a tree. James was picking at the long pieces of grass, "They are having a ball, aren't they?" he asked.

Steph nodded. "So what's it like being an only child? She asked. James leant back against the tree, "Well sometimes it is a bit lonely, but Ash has pretty much always been around, sort of like having a sister," he replied "What about you and Gina, is it weird being a twin?" he asked.

Steph laughed, "More weird than you know. We have this thing where we feel each other's pain."

James looked amazed, "For real, one of you gets hurt, and the other feels the pain?" he asked.

"No, not like that, we both feel the pain. If Gina broke her arm, she would be in pain, and I would be as well. The other person doesn't feel it as strong, and it seems to be acuter the closer we are," Steph replied.

"That's nuts," James stated. Steph grinned, "You don't know the half of it," she thought to herself.

Gina had come up with a sneaky idea of getting Ash to take a photo of the three siblings together. "Hey, how about one with James, Steph and I?" Gina asked after they had made just about every other combination.

Ash readily agreed, "Guess I'm behind the lens then," she added. Gina and Steph stood either side of James as Ash looked through the viewfinder. Ash was astonished, "You three look so alike." She said out loud, as she clicked the shutter.

James looked shocked, "Gee thanks, Ash, what are you saying, I look like a girl?" he asked.

Gina sensing a possible disaster cut in, "Well there are worse things to look like, you could look like a boy," she teased. All four of them ended up rolling on the ground laughing. Ash gave Gina a copy of the image on a USB stick the next day. Gina had it printed and framed for Paula. She and Steph gave it to Paula at dinner that night. "We got this for you Mom," Steph said handing her the wrapped present.

"Oh this is lovely, girls, but my birthday is ages away. What's this for?" Paula asked.

The girls looked at Paula, "No reason, just to say we love you," Gina replied as Paula unwrapped the picture. Paula pulled the remaining paper from the photo and turned it over revealing the three smiling faces.

"Oh, my," Paula said bringing her hand up to her mouth. "It's perfect, you all look so happy." Tears were rolling down Paula's face. "We look happy because that is how we are meant to be Mom." Steph pointed out. "We are happy when we are around him, but it hurts to know that you miss out." Paula rose and hugged the girls; it did hurt not getting to see him but knowing the girls understood made it just a little bit easier to bear.

20

Feb 9, 2013

Paula encouraged the girls to invite James and Ash over Friday night for pizza and a board game. It was a way she could see her son without it looking like she was a stalker. James was now off the crutches, so he and Ash walked over to the Farley's motel. Ash had brought Pictionary with her, having seen how utterly useless the twins were at art she figured she and James had better than even odds at wasting them.

The four kids were crashed out on the floor eating pizza. "I cannot eat another piece." James proclaimed, picking up yet another slice of meat-lovers.

"Well someone needs to feed you, James. Look at you; you're all skin and bone.," Mrs Farley stated. Ash had noticed that Mrs Farley kept looking at James in a bit of a strange way anytime she was around. In fact, she spent most of the time looking at James, and when she noticed Ash looking she would quickly look away. It was just another piece of the puzzle that were the Farley's, that just didn't fit. James began to hiccup.

Ash started to laugh, "Serves you right, stud." was Ash's ever so helpful comment.

"Watch this," James said in between hiccups. Suddenly he stopped, and they all waited for him to start again.

"No way", Ash said, after waiting a few moments for James to restart, "not fair, he does this all the time. He starts hiccupping then he just chooses to stop. It is totally weird, no one else I know can do it!" she explained.

Paula grinned, "It's not that strange? The girls can do that two." Paula said without thinking. "It's a family thing, their granddad could do it, and it used to bug me no end." Paula looked at Ash and realised what she had said. "I guess it is not just our family that can do it then." Paula back-peddled, hoping Ash had missed the slip-up.

"Well how about that game then?" Gina asked trying to cover up for her mum.

"I don't think it is fair that you and Steph are on the same side. You probably read each other's minds." Announced Ash. They all laughed.

"Ok then," Gina said, "I will be on your team, and we can kick Steph and James's buts."

The game hadn't been going on long before James and Steph were miles out in front, it was like they had some mental connection. "Those two must be cheating." Paula spoke up, watching from the sofa, "I think Ash and Steph should play together." she suggested. "Hey, I am in for anything that stops these two cheats," Ash replied. "I agree," Steph added reading her mother's mind.

"Fine, ok," James laughed, "I know when I am not wanted." James switched to Gina, and the game started again, and within moments it was clear that with either James or Steph drawing the other could guess correctly.

"How can you get 'horse' from that?" Ash exclaimed, "3-year-olds draw better than you Kirkland!" The four young people ended up in fits of laughter on the floor.

When Ash and James had left, there was a knock at the door, and in came Dennis. "Dad" both girls exclaimed at once rushing over to give him a hug.

"We thought you couldn't come," Gina said looking at Paula.

Steph gave her mother an accusing look, "You knew!" her accusation was accompanied with a grin.

"I thought it might be a pleasant surprise for us all. I know I said it would be easier without Dennis but I think we might just need him around now." Paula replied.

Dennis moved over to give Paula a big hug. "Oh how I have missed my girls," he exclaimed. "So why do you think you only just need me now?" Dennis asked.

21

They all sat down at the table, and the girls described what had been happening over the last few weeks. Dennis could not believe the luck they had in getting into the same classes, and his jaw dropped when he learned about James and Ash visiting earlier in the night. "I think we might have a small problem," shared Paula. "I think Ash is on to us. She seems to pick up on the most innocent mistakes we make and puts the pieces together. I don't believe she has it all worked out, but I doubt that this ruse is going to hold together much longer." Paula's statement had them all thinking.

"So what do you think we should do about it?" Gina asked.

"I'm not sure honey, I'm not sure. If she figures it out or even asks the wrong questions we might just have a major problem." Paula replied.

"We can't lose him now, Mom, we have got so close. Can't we just tell James the truth?" Steph asked.

Dennis had been sitting quietly listening to what was being said. "You guys think she has an idea that something is fishy huh? Well, the fastest way to stop her fishing for clues is to tell her the truth," Dennis let what he was saying sink in. "The way I figure it is that she is going to catch you out completely sooner or later and tell James. If we control how she finds out, then we might, and it is just might, have a better chance of her being on our side, and then we might be able to control how James finds out. She might even be of some help." Paula reached over and took Dennis's hand

and gave it a squeeze. Dennis looks around at his girls, and they all gave him a little nod.

"So, just how do you propose to tell her?" Steph asked."

"You girls could always tell her at school," Paula suggested.

"No, I think that is a bad idea," voiced Dennis. "She might just go straight to James and tell him or report us all to a teacher. No, if we do this then I think we need to maintain control over the situation." They all sat quietly thinking. "All right then, so to make this work, we need to get her alone to tell her," Gina suggested.

22

Feb 10, 2013

Paula and Dennis sat in Paula's car waiting. Ash had mentioned to Gina that she liked to go for an early morning walk each day while most people were still at home in bed, but they were unsure what time that might be. Dennis was beginning to hate this car, even with the passenger seat pushed all the way back he was still cramped. "We're on a stake out, and you don't bring coffee?" he grumped.

"Oh stop your whining." Paula said laughing, "If you had drunk coffee you would right now need to pee, and the only place to do that would be in a bottle."

Dennis chuckled, "Yea, well I note you didn't bring one of those either." he quipped knowing, that as usual, Paula was right. They have parked about five doors down from Ash's house. Close enough they could see her come out but not so close that she would see the car from her windows. Dennis sat up in his seat, "Is that her?" he asked seeing a young-looking person come out from a house and start out down the street.

"Yes, that's her," Paula was getting excited. Ash was walking towards them and so far had not noticed the car. "Right, here I go," said Paula, "wish me luck." Paula opened the door and headed in the direction of Ash.

Ash hadn't noticed the little red car at all until she saw the door open and a woman wrapped in a warm jacket hopped out. Much to her surprise, the woman turned out to be Mrs Farley. "Um, hi, Mrs Farley," Ash said with evident surprise in her voice. "What are you doing here?"

Paula took a big breath, "Ash there are things you need to know about James, Gina and Steph." If Ash was surprised, she didn't show it now.

Ash spoke up, "Like why all three of them feel pain when one of them gets hurt?" she asked.

It was Paula's turn to be shocked, "You know about that?" she asked, amazed. "I saw it first hand when James had his fall during the race, well I say I saw it, but I am having trouble believing it," Ash replied.

"Ash, my husband and I would like to talk to you somewhere a bit more private, you could choose the location, we don't want to scare you. Perhaps we could meet you there and have a chat?" Paula asked.

"Mrs Farley, James doesn't know anything about this does he?" Ash asked.

Paula swallowed nervously and looked along the street towards the Kirkland house, "No, Ash he doesn't, and if he finds out the wrong way people could get hurt, including him."

Ash looked at Mrs Farley and made a decision, whipping her phone out she dialled her Dad.

"Hey honey what's up?" She heard her father say.

"Hey Dad I have just bumped into the Farley's," Paula's heart sank, Ash was going to dob them in. "They have invited me over for breakfast, so I won't be home for a while," Ash explained.

"No prob, thanks for letting me know, have fun." Her father hung up. Ash registered the shock and relief on Mrs Farley's face and laughed. "Thought I was going to nark, didn't you?" Ash asked. Paula smiled, "Yes Ash I did, hop in."

23

Ash hopped in the back seat and was surprised to see a man sitting in the front. He turned to her and extended his hand, "Hi, I'm Dennis, Gina and Steph's adopted Dad."

"Aren't you forgetting something Dennis?" Paula asked getting behind the wheel.

"Oh, yes, sorry, I'm also Paula's husband." Dennis chuckled.

Paula put the car in gear and turning to Ash said: "So where to?" Paula asked.

"Got any leftover pizza at your motel?" Ash replied, grinning. "Right then, motel it is," Replied Paula, putting the car into gear and driving off.

Paula parked the car outside their motel room, and the three of them got out. This was getting fascinating, Ash thought to herself, hoping that in a few moments she would have the whole story. Paula opened the door stepped inside with Ash and Dennis following her in. Ash could hear singing from the other room, and a shower was running. "Gina shuts up and get out, they're back," Steph yelled at Gina. "Did you have any luck with Ash?" She said walking into her parent's room. Steph must have had the first shower as she still had a towel wrapped around her hair as it dried. "Oh, hey, you're here," Steph gave Ash a hug, "So you know then?" she asked.

"Um no, not really." Ash replied, "I had hoped to get some answers here."

Dennis pulled a chair out from the table for Ash. "How about I fix some breakfast and coffee, and Paula can fill you in?" he asked Ash. "Sounds great." Ash plonked herself down in the offered chair and waited for Paula and Steph to take a seat.

At that moment Gina came through from the adjoining room. "Hi, Ash. Someone making some breakfast?" Gina asked, as she pulled up a seat and joined the others at the table.

"I'm not sure where to begin," Paula said looking at Ash. "I guess I should just come out with the truth. James is my biological son and a triplet to Gina and Steph." Ash sat there with her mouth hanging open.

Ash said nothing for what seemed like ages, "James is your son?" She managed to say after trying to gather her thoughts. "And he was born the same time as Gina and Steph?" Gina and Steph nodded. "But how is that possible? James's parents are Simon and Olivia Kirkland."

Paula took a deep breath and told Ash the full story of how she had got pregnant at seventeen, how her family had cut her off and how she had ended up at a clinic run by Dr Simon Kirkland. She went on to describe how they had taken James from her making her believe he had died. Dennis poured out some coffee for everyone and continued the story about how he had met Paula at University while she was a student. Ash noticed Dennis had turned a bit red while he recounted the story of how they became an item, and she saw the pride in his eyes as he described Paula's efforts as a Mum with two little girls and a full study load on top. She could tell that Dennis and Paula were very much in love. Paula then finished the story with how she had bumped into the nurse who had helped steal James at her local coffee shop and about Nurse Samantha's crisis of conscience that led them to the truth and to their discovery of where James now lived.

Ash sat silently through the whole story not saying a word. When Paula had finished by describing that day at the race, Ash finally spoke up. "It can't be real. I mean it just seems like some plot in a movie, not real life." Paula started to object, but Ash cut her off, "I didn't say I don't believe you, I meant it just seems so surreal. Now it all makes sense, the stupid hiccup thing, the shared pain, the freaky Pictionary skills and the blood type. It just all makes sense," she replied.

Paula looked at Ash, confused, "The blood type? What do you mean?"

Ash grinned, "You don't remember, do you? When you came to school to sign up Steph and Gina. The lady at the counter asked you their blood type. You told her AB-, only just the day before I had been in the hospital with James, I read his chart, and he has the same type. It's rare, and it got me thinking," Ash explained.

Dennis looked over at Paula, "I guess it was a good thing to tell this young lady. It seems to me she would have figured it out pretty soon anyway." he said.

24

"Oh man you have to tell James, he is going to freak!" Ash exclaimed.

Dennis frowned, "That's just the problem Ash, we can't tell James, we need to get some evidence first. Dr Kirkland has made threats in the past, and it looks like James was not the only baby he has stolen. The nurse, Samantha, claims that he may have taken tens of children over the years. We have save James and put a stop to Dr Kirkland's plans," he explained.

Ash sighed, "I don't think any of you understand. James doesn't fit in with his family he hates it there. His father is horrible to him," she explained.

Paula looked suddenly concerned, "Ash, does he abuse him?" she asked.

Ash looked back at Paula, "Not physically, but to the Dr, Kirkland James is just a burden now. Dr Kirkland enjoys the prestige that James brings, but he doesn't care one bit about him. It's all about image to him." Ash could see they didn't follow. "It's like having a fancy car with all the badges removed, to Dr Kirkland the car would be worthless." They were starting to get it Ash could see. "James is successful; he makes Dr Kirkland look good. He pushes James to perform, to be successful because he completes the picture. The reason James is so good at pretty much everything is that he knows he has to be good at everything, nothing else matters to Dr Kirkland."

Paula was stunned. "You mean to say James is nothing more than a trophy to him?" she asked.

"That's exactly what I am saying. Dr Kirkland feeds off the attention James brings, and it doesn't hurt that he is seen as bringing up James himself," replied Ash.

"But what happens if he is not perfect, or if he has a serious accident, what then?" asked Gina.

Ash shook her head, "I don't know, but I doubt he would be of any value to Dr Kirkland anymore. When he blew his hamstring, his father milked it for all it was worth. 'Poor James, didn't he do well, even though he was injured he pushed through.'" Ash mimicked Dr Kirkland perfectly, "He couldn't wait to go into town so people could ask how James was." Ash let her words sink in; she thought she might have laid it on a bit thick but it was the truth, Dr Kirkland didn't love James, not one iota. What he loved was having a successful son who made him look good.

"Ok," said Dennis, "so we agree James is at risk. The big question has to be is he more at risk knowing the truth?" Dennis asked.

"Right now we have no proof of anything." Paula pointed out. Dennis jumped out of his chair, "Oh, I forgot to show you this." Dennis went to his bag, reaching in he brought out a typed and signed document. "We do have some evidence, Samantha has signed an affidavit with her lawyer as a witness, it's not much, but in time it might help convince someone," he explained.

"So do we bring our brother up to speed or leave him in the dark?" Steph asked.

Paula look around the table, "I want him to know the truth so badly." she replied, "But I fear, I am only doing it for me."

Gina gave her a hug, "No Mum, you're not selfish like that, you want the best for James, and that is not Dr Kirkland, it's us!"

Dennis cleared his throat, "I think it still might be a little early to tell James," he declared.

The debate raged backwards and forwards, but in the end, they all came to an agreement. The time was not right to tell James. Ash would help Gina and Steph get closer to James and at the same time try fishing for evidence. It was like positioning the chess pieces on the board. Dennis kept insisting they needed to be ready for when the time was right. Dennis was much happier with this plan even though he knew Paula would just like to snatch James away in the dead of night.

Ash looked at her watch, "Wow, midday, how did that happen. I better be getting home before Dad starts to worry," she exclaimed. Paula grabbed her keys and moved towards the door. "I will drop you home. You girls want to come for a ride?" Paula asked Gina and Steph.

"Why not." They replied in tandem.

They drove off with Ash in the front passenger seat and the twins behind. Ash turned in her seat and looked back at Gina and Steph, "I didn't like you two when we first met," Ash announced, "But I think I have changed my mind."

All four of them laughed, it was a good release of the tension. "Ash," asked Steph, "Does James know you love him?"

Ash stared straight ahead, "You know, I ask myself that question almost every day, and I never seem to get the answer. Sometimes I think James thinks I am his sister. How ironic is that?" Ash replied laughing.

Gina leant forward and touched Ash on the shoulder, "I think he loves you, but he's afraid to show it, he might be scared he will turn out like Dr Kirkland," Gina remarked.

"Hey," Paula quipped, "seems we got the room for at least one more, want to be Gina and Steph's sister as well?"

Ash just about wet herself laughing; this family was so unlike James's, full of laughter and fun. She was busting to tell him, but this secret would have to wait. "Has anyone told you guys you're all nuts?" Ash asked grinning.

Paula answered, "All the time, Ash, all the time."

25

James handed his Father the sealed letter from the school. He had no idea what the letter contained and to break the seal would have been considered a cardinal sin. His father liked to order him around, so James stood patiently waiting to be dismissed. "Ah, yes!" Dr Kirkland exclaimed, "they are finally going to formally open the new library, and they have invited us as guests. Mrs Jones has asked if I would give a speech in honour of our donation. This is none too soon; you have all been using that 'new' library for over six months. It is the time it had a proper formal opening," he exclaimed.

Nothing pleased Dr Kirkland more than attention like this. As far as he was concerned, the honour was his to give the school not the other way around, but that mattered little as he would happily give the speech as it would show how important the Kirkland family was in Greenspan.

James cleared his throat, "Mrs Jones has asked me to pass on a message to you in person," James announced. "She said that you might want to attend opening as there will be a prize giving for the Laker maths award."

Kirkland knew that Mrs Jones was sending him a message, the message was that James had won the award. Yes, thought Kirkland, that would look good, his son being presented with the Laker Prize, the boy was working out very well. Dr Kirkland looked at Jame with a slight smile forming, "James, please tell Mrs Jones that I would be delighted to attend and I am honoured to be invited to give a speech. That will be all." Dr Kirkland dismissed James much the way one might reject a stray dog. As James turned to leave, he noticed the family painting was hanging slightly off centre on the wall. James grinned to himself, bet that doesn't stay like that for long. 'Dr Perfect' will fix that right away, he thought, with a smirk, as he left the room. At least if he won the maths prize, it would keep his father off his back for a while. Nothing seemed to make his father as happy as good results, more importantly, nothing made Dr Kirkland more comfortable than when James was the best at whatever he was doing.

Paula had started in earnest looking at antiques in Greenspan. Texas was not short of stores selling fine antiques, but that was not the kind of store Paula liked. The best kind of stores, for her, were the ones that sold second-hand goods. They often had absolute gems hiding in dusty corners. Often all the item or items needed was a bit of a clean to bring them back to their former glory. Today had been frustrating, several small stores had cottoned on to her innocent shopper routine and were now bargaining hard. Word had got around that a woman in her thirties was buying up loads of old items and shipping them off. That said she had still managed to come away with three vases that, with a touch of love, would provide her with a good profit. Paula arrived back to the motel. This whole thing was taking longer than she planned. She thought to herself. And living out of a motel room is not my style.

Gina and Steph were sitting at the table completing some homework. It amazed Paula how well they had slotted into Greenspan High; Ash had helped. The four of them had formed a special bond. Paula thought to herself. "Hey guys, what do you think about us renting a place here in town for a while?" Paula asked.

Gina and Steph looked up, "It would make our cover story a bit more believable," Steph acknowledged. "By the way Mum, how are we affording all this?"

Paula remained amazed how one moment the girls could come up with very complex ideas on getting James back, and the next, well, how they could not even think about the cost of this little endeavour. "While you two have been swanning around at school, I have been out buying antiques and sending them back to the studio. With the number of stores here and the quality of the antiques, we had done better than when we were back home. If this keeps up, I might just rent somewhere here to live." she advised.

"Well since you seem to think we have been swanning around at school I guess you don't want coming to the opening of the new library, where Gina and I 'might' be getting a prize," Steph suggested grinning.

Paula looked at her two daughters. "I guess a low profile just got knocked off the list then." Paula laughed.

Steph looked over at her mother, "Well what can we say, Mom? You can't keep a good thing down."

"Good things," Gina interjected.

"Yes, you can't keep a 'couple' of good things down." Steph finished for the two of them, grinning.

Paula looked pleased, like any proud parent would, "So what is this award for, that you two 'swans' have managed to get?" she asked.

"The Laker Prize, for math. We entered, well they sort of force all the kids to enter, and won it." Gina said simply.

"Figures," Paula thought to herself, "the twins were always good at math, it just seemed to come very naturally to them." "Ok, I'll come and be the proud parent. Just remember we are trying to keep a low profile so no solving world peace or nuclear fission while we are still here." Gina and Steph both laughed. Paula, on the other hand, thought she might as well be telling the wind not to blow. She had to remind herself that her girls were chronic overachievers and liked not only to compete with other students but also with each other. The competition could be fierce, but each child always supported the other win or lose.

"So when is this famous library opening then?" Paula asked. "7:00 pm Friday, so Dad won't be able to come," Gina said forlornly. "Your Dad has been to plenty of these things in the past, missing this one won't kill him, or you girls for that matter." Paula was touched, Gina and Steph never treated Dennis like a step-father. To them, he was their father, and that was that. It made Paula smile to think of her mixed up crazy family and the love they shared. In the back of her mind, Paula knew that telling James was only going to max out the mixed up crazy part, but she also knew that there was plenty of love left in this family for him too.

26

"So, I hear you have competition for the Laker prize," Gina told James as he placed a steel nail into the beaker of copper sulphate. Gina could see the look of surprise through his safety glasses.

"Really, what have you heard?" James asked, the edge of tension in his voice was barely hidden. What would his father say if he didn't get the prize?

"Rumour has it that it was a three horse race and it was close." Gina was enjoying making her brother squirm; she had never had one to tease before.

"Do you know which of them won?" James asked trying to come across casually.

Gina grinned, "Yip, I know all of them, three-way tie. Steph overheard the office lady talking about how strange it was for them to have to give it to three people."

James looked straight at Gina, "Please tell me the other two winners are not you and Steph, cause I am pretty sure I am one of them," he remarked.

Gina laughed, "You have a problem sharing the stage with a set of twin girls?" she asked, in mock surprise.

James looked at the back of the room where Ash and Steph were conducting the same experiment. "No, I just don't think it is fair, you two probably have some weird metal link and compared the answers or something."

Gina punched him in the arm, "Ow!," he exclaimed, rubbing where Gina had hit. Gina could see Steph out of the corner of her eye rubbing the same spot. She also desperately wanted to rub her arm that was throbbing in unison with her brother's and sister's but dared not to in case she gave their secret away.

Paula had decided to dress up a bit for the prize giving. Searching through the little selection of clothes she had managed to bring along did not yield the best of choices, but she would just have to make do. Paula ended up choosing a pair of tan coloured dress slacks with a brown suede jacket over a cream blouse. Rounding out the outfit was a pair of brown cowboy boots she had found, in a store in the mall, just that morning, fitting she thought, considering the state they were living in.

Paula knocked on the girl's door and went in. Gina and Steph were lying on their beds already dressed. It always amazed Paula how they could carry off the classy casual look. Both wore jeans of different tones, but they had each worn a simple white top. Their individuality showed in the jackets they had each chosen. Gina had gone with a luxurious red leather jacket Paula and Dennis had got her for her 16th birthday. Steph was wearing a mustard yellow jacket out of corduroy, with oversized buttons. Both had their hair tied back in simple ponytails. "Don't you two look good," Paula exclaimed. "Thanks, Mom, not bad yourself," Gina replied.

"We better get going if we are not going to be late," Paula said heading for the door.

James hated these events. Firstly his father insisted on him going formal. Pressed black pants with a button down business shirt and a tie. The worst part was Dr Kirkland would not let him stand near Ash. He would have had a heart attack if someone got a photo of James and Ash together at an event like this.

Ash decided she would dress up, but her idea of dress up was typically black pants with, you guessed it a black top. For formal occasions, Ash would wear something with buttons on the top. A casual glance towards Ash's shoes would reveal a pair of cherry red Doc. Martin boots.

James stood beside his father looking for anyone he could escape with, Ash, Gina, Steph, anyone. Right now he was so desperate he might even submit to the Jones leading him away. Dr Kirkland spent most of his time fussing with his tie, telling James not to fidget, and explaining how important it was that the family image was not tarnished. All the while keeping a wary eye out for Ash so he could manoeuvre James away if 'that girl' got too close for comfort. It was getting close to the time his father would give his speech when James noticed Gina and Steph come in the library followed by Mrs Farley. James gave them a quick wave and a look of 'save me.' Sensing James's need the girls pulled Paula over towards James and Dr Kirkland.

Paula's heart froze as James ushered them over to him and Dr Kirkland. This was the first time Paula had seen the man who had stolen her child. She fought the instinct to slap Dr Kirkland across the face. James managed the introductions, "Dad this is Gina, Steph and their Mom Paula." Paula extended her hand "Mr Kirkland, so nice to meet you. James has told us so much about you." Paula said while lying on both counts. "Oh it's Dr Kirkland, Paula was it? I can't pick the accent, but you're not from around these parts are you?" Dr Kirkland asked.

"No sadly we had only just moved to the area about four weeks ago, we hailed from Denver before that." Paula knew how this game was going to be played; it was to be a game of 'one-up-man-ship'.

"Ms Farley sells antiques," James explained to his father.

Paula nodded, "Well I do sell the odd item, but most of my work is in restoration, you know, correcting the neglect that some people treat their possessions with." Paula went on, "You would simply not believe what some people do to the most valuable items they own Dr Kirkland." Paula's double meaning few over his head, but not the twins'.

"Yes, no doubt it is more common with those with 'new money'." Dr Kirkland stated.

Paula faked a brilliant smile, "Unfortunately the abuse of one's powers is not limited to old or new money Dr Kirkland," she said. Keeping up this act of being nice was taxing her composure. She had had enough of this man and wanted James as far away from him as soon as possible. Paula addressed James, "Would you be a dear and show us to the drinks table? It was lovely meeting you, Dr Kirkland." Paula lied.

James lead them over towards the drinks table. "I am very sorry my father was so rude, Mrs Farley." James apologised handing the girls and Paula a drink.

"No need to apologise, James, one cannot pick their parents and some parents should never have been picked." Paula's pronouncement had James confused, but before he could ask what she meant Principal Jones tapped on the microphone.

27

"Can I have your attention please?" Principal Jones asked, coming up onto the makeshift stage that had been installed at the end of the library. "I would like to take this opportunity to welcome you all here to the official opening of our new school library. Our wonderful school has so many excellent facilities and the addition of this new building will only further enhance our reputation as the top high school in Texas." Principal Jones paused as the crowd clapped in agreement. "I would now like to invite our honoured guest, Dr Simon Kirkland, to say a few words on behalf of all those that donated funds towards the building of our new library. After this speech there will be a special presentation of the Laker Prize for Mathematics" Principal Jones moved away from the microphone as Dr Kirkland took the stage to the scattered applause from the crowd.

If someone had asked Paula what Dr Kirkland had said in his seven-minute speech, she could not have told you. From the moment he took the stage Paula's eyes never left him. It was as though she was sending Dr Kirkland a challenge. Red hot hatred caused through Paula's veins and it took all of her self-control not to shout him down

here in front of all the people. James sensed something was amiss and noticed Gina and Steph standing very close to their mother. James watched as one of Paula's hands sought out Gina's then her other found Steph's. It was like the twins had formed a protective shield around Paula and this all had something to do with his father. What the hell was going on here? What has Mrs Farley got against my dad? Surely the little tat before was not the cause of this?

James asked himself. No, what James could see was pure hatred.

Ash saw the scene unfold and watching James she realised that he had noticed the change in Paula and the girls reaction. He has to be told! She told herself. Ash moved slowly towards James and when she managed to get alongside he noticed her. Ash nodded towards Paula and the twins. So Ash had seen it as well, James thought to himself. He took a moment to glance around to see if anyone else had noticed, but most people were looking up at his father.

Ash leant in and whispered in James's ear, "We need to talk, I will explain it all later." Indicating in Paula and the girl's direction.

Dr Kirkland was in his element, on stage with a captive audience hanging on his every word. He had rehearsed this speech countless times to get it just right. He looked around the audience ensuring that he made eye contact with all the most important figures but skipping those he did not know. As his eyes moved towards the drinks table, he caught sight of his son. James was standing near the Farley woman and her teenage daughters. The woman was staring right at him with unblinking eyes. He looked away and almost lost his place. Getting back to his speech he intentionally avoided looking over at the woman as he felt a small shiver of fear run up his spine, but for the life of him, he could not place why. He was sure he had seen her before, but right now, in front of all these people, he could not for the life of himself remember where he had seen her before. As the applause died off, he made his way off the stage.

Principal Jones took to the stage again, "Thank you, Dr Kirkland, what a wonderful guest we have had to our official opening," gushed Principal Jones to another round of applause from the crowd. "I would now like to call up the winners of this year's Laker Prize for Mathematics. Please note, that was no mistake ladies and gentlemen, I did say winners, as for the first time, we have had a three-way tie for first place." Applause filled the library. "Please put your hands together for our three winners, James Kirkland, Gina Farley and Stephanie Farley." The crowd clapped, and some of the students cheered and whooped as James, Gina and Steph took to the stage to receive their prize.

28

Paula looked up at her three children standing there, on the stage. They were all winners and tears began to run down her face. Ash pressed a tissue into Paula's hand and whispered: "I know you're feeling emotional, but you need to tone it down."

Paula sniffed back some more tears and gave Ash's hand a quick squeeze. "I never thought I would see them all together like this," Paula whispered to Ash.

"It's time we told James," Ash declared, "He has the right to know." Paula nodded, feeling the relief that was coming soon.

Simon Kirkland joined Principal Jones. He would need to speak to James to see if had scored one hundred percent. If he had then, he could hardly be angry at him for coming first equal. On the other hand, he mused, if James's score had not been perfect, well then he would be sure to let him, and the teaching staff at Greenspan High know. "I think I know that woman from somewhere," Simon stated, indicating towards Paula.

"I wouldn't think so Dr Kirkland, they have only just moved into the area." Principal Jones replied.

"How do you know that?" Simon asked, getting annoyed. "I was the one who interviewed them when she and her daughters moved here." She was getting annoyed at all the attention Simon was giving the other winners.

"Did she tell you her first name?" Simon asked getting more annoyed at Principal Jones disinterest. "I think she said it was Philippa or something like that." Neither Farley or Philippa rang any bells for Simon, but he was confident that he had seen the woman before. If he could only manage to remember where.

James was confused; Ash had said she would explain, but right now he was stuck with his father as he dragged him from person to person to be congratulated. James was sick of this, he felt he should be pleased that he had won, but as usual his father was turning this into something about himself. James was just the window dressing on his professional life.

"Dad, I need to use the bathroom," James managed to say between two groups of good-wishers.

"Ok, but don't be too long, we have not seen the Chair of the School Board yet," Kirkland replied.

James headed towards the bathroom, looking for Ash. As he rounded the corner, she grabbed him and pulled him aside. "Ash, what the hell is going on?" James hissed.

Ash leant closer to James, "We can't talk here, come over to my place after you get home tonight, we can talk there," Ash replied. "I've got to go, see you later."

James was getting confused now, the brief chat with Ash had left him with far more questions and not a single answer.

Ash walked back out to the library to find Gina and Steph. They were standing talking to their mother as Ash approached, "James suspects something is up," she explained. "He saw the thing with the three of you, I think he might have even felt protective towards Paula like Gina and Steph did, but I doubt he knew why he felt that way."

Paula rubbed her temples, "This is a disaster, I think Dr Kirkland may have recognised me. We are going to have to tell James and soon before he finds out some other way." Paula explained.

Ash could see that Paula was in no shape to make decisions, so she took charge, "I've spoken to James and told him to come and see me at my house after he gets home. I think Gina and Steph should be there." Ash stated.

"What about your Dad? Won't he be at home?" Paula asked.

"No, not tonight, he has the night shift," Ash replied directly. "He won't be back until the early hours of tomorrow morning."

This was all going far too fast for Paula. She kept trying to think of reasons not to tell James and kept coming up blank. All of the reasons paled in comparison to what might happen if Dr Kirkland had recognised her. No, they had to move tonight, they might already be too late, Paula thought. "Ok, we do it tonight. I will drop you girls off at Ash's house. Call me when you need me to pick you up," she said.

Gina stepped over to her mum, "Are you going to be ok by yourself?" she asked.

Paula was touched by her daughter's concern and gave Gina a big hug, "I'll be fine, just be careful and call me when you need me, ok?" she asked.

Ash start to fidget, "We better get going if we are to meet James at my place" Ash replied.

29

Paula watched the girls go inside Ash's house. As she drove away, her phone rang. "Hey," Dennis' voice came down the line, "Where are you guys? I'm at the motel," he announced.

"You're here?" Paula exclaimed. "Oh thank God, I'm on my way back now, I will tell you everything when I get back."

"Ok, see you soon Paula," Dennis replied, unsure what was going down.

Paula hung up and with a sigh of relief drove home to the motel, At least I don't have to wait alone. She thought to herself as she drove back to the motel.

Dennis sat in his rental car waiting for Paula to arrive. She was obviously upset, and it was hard having to wait to hear what was causing it. Some of him wanted to ring her back and find out over the phone, but he knew that Paula would never do that. No, he would just have to wait to see what was eating her up.

It had taken over an hour for James and his father to get home; there had been plenty more people to thank and shake hands with. James excused himself from his father and went upstairs to bed. He knew that his father would soon be in bed and sound asleep. The waiting, however, was torture, James looked out his window and could see Ash's window three houses over. The light was on, and he knew that Ash would also be busting a gut waiting. The sound of snoring came from down the hallway from his father's room. James quietly opened his window and looked down the ivy-covered trellis. Damn, Ash makes this look easy. If I die doing this I am going to kill her; he thought to himself as he climbed down. The trip to Ash's house took only two minutes, but to James, it felt like an hour. Just as he went to knock on the front door, it opened.

Ash was standing there in her pyjamas, "What do you want at this late hour, Mr Kirkland?" Ash grinned, "Get inside, you idiot, people will talk." she ordered.

James relaxed, Perhaps this is not some grand conspiracy, after all, he thought. "Where's Detective Scott?" James asked.

"Night shift" Ash replied "Come on up to my room," Ash locked the door, and James followed her up the stairs. Ash opened her bedroom door, and there sitting on her bed was Gina and Steph.

The hairs on the back of James' neck stood on end. "Ok, so what the hell is going on?" he asked, his defences up, as he remained in the doorway. Ash pulled him into the room and closed the door.

Gina was the first to speak and cut straight to the point, "James, the Kirkland's are not your real parents!"

30

Gina let the statement hang in the air as James looked at each of the girls. He could see no sign of humour or prank; the girls looked deadly serious. "And how exactly do you know they are not my parents?" James asked.

Steph looked over at Gina and Gina nodded, "Perhaps we should tell you the whole story before you ask any more questions." Steph replied. James looked to Ash, a girl he had known almost all his life, a girl who he knew would not joke about something like this, a girl who he completely, totally trusted. Ash took James's hand and led him to a chair. She kept on holding his hand after he sat down.

"James, this is an affidavit from the nurse that helped deliver you when you were born. She worked for your father. You father was stealing babies and selling them to wealthy families."

Gina passed James a copy of the affidavit as Steph continued, "Your Mum, the one who died when you were eight, was not your real mum. Your real Mum was told you had died at birth, and she did not find out the truth until quite recently."

To James, this all sounded insane. "So who is my real mother then?" he asked, half joking.

"Her maiden name was Paula Johnson, and she was only seventeen when she had you and two other babies," Steph paused, "James, you were born one of three triplets, there were you and twin girls. Gina and I are your sisters." There it was, Gina thought, Steph had just dropped the bombshell.

James stared at Gina and Steph as if they were crazy but somewhere deep inside it started to make sense, but he was not yet entirely convinced, he was torn. James had loved his mother, and she had loved him, of that he was sure. "What proof do you have?" James demanded. Gina looked at Steph and nodded, Steph reached up to a poster on Ash's wall and pulling a drawing pin out suddenly jabbed it into her leg. Both Gina and James shouted out in pain. "What the heck!" James yelled, rubbing his leg.

Gina was rubbing her leg as well as she looked at her brother, "James do you remember having a sore arm when you were eight?" Gina asked still rubbing her leg. James nodded slowly; he did remember that it was not long before his mother had died. Both his parents had thought he was putting it all on because the doctor could not find anything wrong. Gina continued, "I broke my arm. I fell off the climbing bars at school. It was sometime in July, and I could not go swimming because of the cast," she explained.

"We all have a connection because we are related, brother and sisters, we're triplets" Steph added.

James slumped back into the chair. His mind was racing, it all seemed too crazy to be true, but deep down, way down, he knew what they had told him was right, they did have a connection, some of this did make sense. "I need a few moments to think," He replied. Gina, Steph and Ash stood to leave. "Can you stay?" James asked directing the question to Ash. She nodded as Gina and Steph closed the door behind them and went downstairs to wait. Ash looked at James; she could see the turmoil raging inside him as he stood and began to pace around his room. "This is crazy!" James exclaimed, "I can't be related to them. My parents are Simon and Olivia Kirkland…" his speech trailed off as he began to weep. "She loved me; I always thought she loved me."

Ash realised James was speaking about Olivia. She cleared her throat, "I think she did love you. From what you have told me, you were the most important thing in the world to her," she let the statement hang. "But your father has never loved you. You are their lost brother James; you just need to get over the shock of finding out. Did you know the three of you share the same blood type? You know AB-, the rare one," She added.

James crashed back into his chair. "Do you know what you are asking me to believe?" he asked.

Ash nodded, "I know it seems nuts but, they have nothing to gain from this. It's not about money or some inheritance. I believe they only want the best for you. Paula, your mum, uplifted the family to come and look for you as soon as she found out. James, can't you see they are doing it for you?" James nodded slowly; he was getting it, but it was still a huge thing to take in.

James stood up, "Come on." he said heading for the door. Ash looked surprised, "Come on, where?" she asked. James half grinned nervously, "I think it's the time I met my mother, don't you think?" he replied as he opened the door.

Gina and Steph had sat downstairs on the sofa waiting. "Well, that went well," Steph exclaimed.

Gina looked at her sister, "How exactly, did you expect it to go? I thought he took it pretty well considering," she replied.

Steph sighed, "Yea, suppose you're right; he could have kicked us out of the house and gone straight to his dad. He did feel the pain, though, that has to count for something," Steph acknowledged. Gina rubbed her leg in the spot that Steph had stabbed herself. "Well yes about that, did you have to make the point that hard?" she asked.

Steph grinned, "Oh I think it was just hard enough…" Steph didn't finish, James and Ash were coming down stairs. Ash looked over at Gina and Steph and gave them a subtle thumbs up. Gina and Steph looked back to James, what they saw was exhaustion, he looked like he had run an emotional marathon but as he looked back at the twins a small smile lit up his face.

"You understand," Gina exclaimed and crashed hugged James when he reached the bottom of the stairs. Steph joined her brother and sister in a huge hug. After a few moments, James cleared his throat, "I wondered if we could go visit my mum?"

Gina and Steph started crying. "Oh man, Mom is going to freak," Gina exclaimed.

31

Paula sat clutching the cup of coffee. The tension in the room was tangible. Dennis sat quietly next to Paula. She had a gone through almost all the emotions since arriving home. There had been the worry that Kirkland had recognised her, Anger at what he had done, and now she was racked with fear and doubt about what the girls were trying to do. "I should have told him, Dennis. I sent the girls to do what I should have done," She sobbed. "What kind of mother sends her daughters to do that? Dennis knew that this was not one of those times to try and fix it. Paula just needed to talk and sob it out.

Suddenly the door to the motel room opened, and Gina and Steph walked in. "How did you get here? I thought I was going to come and pick you up?" Paula asked wiping away some tears.

"We got a taxi," Gina replied, "It would have been hard to fit all four of us in your little car," she explained. At that moment James entered the room behind the twins.

Paula stood up and made a sudden audible inhale of breath. "He knows? You know?" she asked, her voice hardly above a whisper. James nodded and with tears streaming down his face started walking towards Paula. Paula ran to James and hugged him like she would never let go. Paula and James were suddenly joined by Gina and Steph and the tears were streaming down their faces as well. Ash stood by the open door watching the reunion unfold. This was the right thing to do, she thought, screw it if Dr Kirkland gets away, they need each other more than revenge.

Dennis walked over to James and extended his hand, "Hi James, I'm Paula's husband and the girl's stepdad, Dennis." James shook his hand in reply.

"We kidnapped him and made him our new dad," Steph exaggerated, grinning.

"Well you two did capture my heart," Dennis said in reply. It was a rare moment when Dennis managed to make his girls speechless like this.

Both Gina and Steph stood up and gave him a huge hug, "We love you, dad!" Steph replied. It had taken a while before any sign of normality returned. Paula kept holding James' hand as though letting it go would mean she might lose him again all the while dabbing her eyes with a handkerchief Dennis had provided.

After a while, James turned to Paula and asked, "What's my real name?"

Paula squeezed his hand. "It's Daniel, your real name is Daniel Seth Johnson," she replied crying.

It was 2 am before Paula, dropped James and Ash back to Ash's house. During the night they had worked out a plan, and it involved James returning to the Kirkland's. Paula was totally against it, but James was insistent. He wanted to find some evidence to convict Dr Kirkland and put an end to his activities once and for all. The whole plan hinged on Paula having not been identified. Paula had only agreed when James suggested that at the first sign the plan had failed, they would all leave town together immediately. The hardest part of the scheme was the Farley's not being able to be with Daniel. Paula seemed to be suffering the worst. She had only just got Daniel back, and now she had to send him into harm's way. But Daniel was insistent; it appeared that it was not just Gina and Steph that had inherited Paula's stubborn genes.

32

James climbed the trellis up to his room and quietly closed his window behind him. The night had been insane, and he highly doubted sleep would come quickly. Although he could not be bothered getting changed, James took off his clothes choosing to sleep in his boxer shorts and a t-shirt. The last thing he needed right now were questions about why he was sleeping in his clothes. As James lay down under his sheets, his thoughts returned to Gina, Stephanie and his real mother Paula. He had spent less than four hours with his real family and yet to James they felt more real than the thousands of hours he had spent here. His true family needed evidence, and he was going to find it. James racked his brain for ideas on where they could start looking. Eventually, the need for sleep overcame the excitement, and he slept.

Daniel awoke late the next morning to his father banging on his door, "James get up, it's 9:45. That girl's here from down the road," Kirkland's voice came through the door.

Daniel sat up in bed and rubbed his head as Ash barged into his room.

"It's ok Mr K. He's not naked," Ash called out the door.

He could just imagine the horrified look on his father's face as he retreated down the stairs. "Please tell me that was all a weird dream last night," Daniel moaned pulling the sheets over his head.

"Nope, it all happened sport. You think the old man recognised Paula?" Ash asked while looking down out the door, to ensure Dr Kirkland was out of earshot.

Daniel pulled back the covers and shook his head. "No, But I don't think this is the safest place to discuss such things, do you think?" Daniel cautioned.

"Totally agree, that's why you need to go on a 'rehabilitation' walk each day. Got to get you back up to speed champ." Ash winked. "Good plan, best I get up then," Daniel announced.

Ash stood by the door looking at Daniel. "Waiting for something?" She asked looking straight at Daniel.

"Yea, how about some privacy," Daniel replied.

"Sugar, I have seen it before, and I know you better than you. How about I turn around and not look, that make you feel better?" Ash asked.

Daniel groaned, "Fine, do that then." Ash turned away from Daniel as he got out of bed, but she could just see him in the reflection in his mirror. Ash grinned as she watched James discard his t-shirt and pull on another. Yes, she thought, I have seen it all before, but that doesn't mean I don't mind seeing it again.

Daniel and Ash went downstairs and headed for the kitchen. Dr Kirkland was sitting reading the business section of the newspaper at the kitchen table. "So you have finally decided to join us then," Dr Kirkland growled.

"Morning sir," Daniel replied, ignoring the jibe from his father. "I think I need to get back into training or I will never be fit enough for the Spring comps," Stated James.

"How are you going to do that? You're not supposed to be running yet James?" Dr Kirkland asked lowering his paper.

"Ash thought it would be a good idea for me to start back easy, by doing some walking," Daniel replied.

Dr Kirkland would not usually agree with anything that Ash suggested, but this was the best way to slowly get James back to normal. "Fine but I better see you doing it every day. I don't want to catch you slacking off!" Dr Kirkland stated. "I think you got your injury because you didn't take your training seriously James, and that is not going to happen again," Kirkland declared.

"Yes, sir." Replied Daniel, "I think I will get started now if that's ok?"

"What about your breakfast?" Dr Kirkland asked.

"Better off not trying to do exercise on a full stomach," Daniel replied.

"Alright then, see you later," Kirkland replied returning to his newspaper. Daniel and Ash slipped out of the kitchen as quickly as possible wanting to avoid any further confrontation.

"So," Daniel asked, as they were leaving the house, "Did you have anywhere in particular in mind for this little 'walk'?"

"I thought the library to do some research, but first I think we should go and wake up the sleeping beauties as they are sure to want to come along," replied Ash.

"Across town, that's quite a walk," James replied.

"Afraid of some exercise champ?" Ash joked.

33

Dr Kirkland walked out and collected the mail from the mailbox. Hmm, he said to himself as he thumbed through the general collection of bank statements, bills and junk mail, then a yellow envelope caught his attention. Dr Kirkland turned and took all the mail back inside, and immediately went to his study. Leaving the yellow letter on his desk, he retrieved his key and locked the door. Dr Kirkland returned to his desk. Using an ornate letter opener in the shape of a Persian sword he opened the letter. His heart always ran a bit quicker when he received a yellow letter. He retrieved the letter from the envelope and had a quick read of the contents. The message was short and straightforward.

> "Dear Sir, after careful consideration of your offer we would like to proceed with your proposal at your earliest opportunity. We have made the agreed deposit into your account in confirmation of the contract.
>
> Regards Carl and Debra Fletcher."

Dr Kirkland allowed himself a rare smile. The Fletchers had decided to go ahead with an ‘adoption'. Kirkland logged onto his personal computer and connected to his office server. He needed to review how many potential targets he had. "Damn," he said out loud. There were no multiple births currently in the system. Although it annoyed Simon to have to wait, he was a patient man, and history had taught him that the ‘next multiple' would not be too far away. History, that word suddenly reminded Simon of the woman at the prize giving. He was sure he and seen her before, but where? Simon glanced down at the yellow page and envelope, remembering they needed to be locked away. As Simon filled them in the safe one of his early notebooks dropped out. Rather than returning it to the safe Simon took it back to his desk. The woman had twins he remembered; they would be about the same age as James give or take. He told himself, that should narrow it down." Simon turned to the pages recording the 2007 births. It was a smaller list with only two entries, the first name stood out, Paula Johnson. Triplets, Two Girls - Gina Dawn Johnson & Stephanie Alice Johnson. One Boy (removed) James Kirkland. Alongside each child Dr Kirkland had made entries such as height and weight etc.

Simon could not for the life of himself remember the names of the twins who came first equal and Principal Jones had said the woman's name was Philippa. Simon was unsure. Picking up his phone, he dialled the school's number. "Thank you for calling Greenspan High school. You have called us after hours; our regular hours are 7:30 am to 6:00 pm Monday to Friday." Simon slammed the phone back into its cradle. He would need to wait until Monday to get any further with this mystery.

34

"So crazy twelve hours then?" Ash commented as she and Daniel walked over to the motel.

"You could say," Daniel replied. "Ash, how long have you known?" Ash had known this question would come. "You know the other week when we hung out at the motel playing games?" She asked. "You knew then?" Daniel was surprised.

"Well not that night, but I noticed some stuff, and Paula saw me seeing. She and Dennis sort of kidnapped me the next morning and told me everything." Daniel didn't say a word but kept walking. Ash grabbed his jacket and pulled him around to face her. "I didn't tell you because we were trying to protect you, we had no evidence. Think about it for a moment. We tell you, you tell your dad, he bolts and we all lose you for good," Ash retorted.

"Sorry," Daniel replied, "It's just pissed me off a bit to be the central piece in a chess game and not even know about it. It makes me feel used."

Ash turned on him, "Damn it, Daniel, don't you get it. This is all happening because they love you, and they're not the only ones. Do you realise that if Paula had found you happy and healthy, she would have just been content to meet you?" Ash was pissed now, "Come on let's go," Ash said continuing to walk.

The rest of the walk was completed in silence. Daniel kept swinging between being thankful and annoyed. Ash stayed annoyed. They arrived at the motel and knocked on

Paula's door. "Oh, Daniel," Paula excitedly said, "come in. What are you both doing here?" she asked.

"Thought I would bring brain dead back here so we could do some research at the library with Gina and Steph," Ash replied.

Paula looked at Ash and Daniel, "Um, is something wrong guys?" Paula asked, looking worried.

"Nope, I think I'm just going to get some air," Ash banged the door closed and went and sat outside.

Paula looked at Daniel, "What did you do?" she asked with a knowing voice.

"Me? I just told her that I was pissed off being the last to know. Ever since then I have been getting the cold shoulder." James replied slumping into a chair at the table. Hearing Daniel, Gina and Steph rushed into the room, "Daniel." they both called and rushed up to him and gave him a hug.

"Gina, Steph, could you give James, oh gosh, I mean Daniel, and I a couple of minutes?" The girls nodded and headed back to their room and closed the door. "Watch this," Paula whispered, as she tiptoed to the door and yanked it open suddenly. The two girls spilt out on the carpeted floor. "Back to your room, and no listening at the door!" Paula ordered.

"Sorry." was the joint reply as the closed the door for the second time. The moment brought a small smile to Daniels' face.

Paula sat down at the table next to Daniel. "That's what you get for having sisters. Go easy on Ash; she has risked her friendship telling you; it could have gone very badly for her. She noticed stuff that we weren't even aware we were doing, but she was smart enough to tell us and not Dr Kirkland. That has to count for something," Paula explained, patting Daniel on the hand.

"I know, I just feel like an idiot for not knowing," Daniel admitted. "Try being told your son is dead and then not insisting on seeing the body," Paula replied. "Do you know how much I regret not doing that simple little thing? I have missed sixteen years of you in my life." Daniel realised how much this could have cost them all. "Paula, I mean mum, I feel like I am stuck between you and Olivia, my old mum. I know I belong to you, but I feel like I owe her. She loved me, I am sure of that, but how could someone that loves you do something like that?" Daniel asked.

Paula sighed, in her head, she wanted to hate Olivia Kirkland, but Daniel was the living evidence that she had loved him. Paula could not attribute all of Daniel's personality to just nature, there had to be some positive nurture there as well and it sure as mud hadn't come from Dr Kirkland. "Daniel, I can't explain how your mother, how Olivia, justified stealing you, but I do believe she loved you. You have turned out to be such a lovely young man. That didn't just come from your genes; she must have had a part in that," she replied.

Daniel nodded as Paula went on. "Loving Olivia is natural, and I understand why you do. You have no reason to feel shame for loving someone that loved you," Paula changed tack, "Daniel, how much do you like Ash?" she asked.

Daniel was stunned, "Like Ash? She's like the sister I have never had. Of course, I like her." Daniel replied, his head tilted towards the table. Paula reached across with her hand and gently lifted Daniels face until he was looking straight at her, "What about more than a sister?" Paula asked, holding his gaze. Daniel looked stunned. "I think Ash loves you."

Paula patted his hand while Daniel continued to sit there with a stunned look on his face. Paula got up, "Now I guess that you have not had breakfast yet, huh? So I am going to do what any good mother does and make her son breakfast, I just have a little catching up to do, sixteen years worth," Paula smiled. "While I get you something to eat there's a young lady outside I think you need to speak to." Paula turned her back to Daniel as she started fussing over making breakfast, fighting the urge to have a good cry. Men could be so darn stupid, missing all the hints a woman could give, but that didn't stop her loving her men just the same.

35

Daniel had never had so much care and compassion heaped on him in one go. In a bit of a daze, he rose and went and put his hand on the door. "Um, Paula, I mean Mom?" Paula looked up from her breakfast prep to Daniel. "Thanks," Daniel said quietly, as he went outside. Sitting outside on a bench was Ash and Dennis. Dennis had a bag of groceries sitting at his feet. "Hi, Daniel." He said holding out his hand, "Sorry I wasn't here to greet you, but the boss sent me out for breakfast supplies. You two staying for a feed?"

Daniel nodded, "We'll be in a moment." Daniel said indicating he and Ash needed to chat.

"Alright see you in a few." Dennis stood up, grabbed the groceries and headed for the door. When the door had closed, Daniel sat down next to Ash. "I need to apologise, I have been a jerk, and you don't deserve to be treated that way," Daniel explained.

Ash sighed, "I did it for you, James," She replied, her anger evaporating from his apology.

"I know, and I get it now. Ash, I love you, I don't know anyone else who would have done this for me." Ash began to reply, but Daniel interrupted. "No, I have something else to say. You always ask why I don't date all the hot girls in school, well the real reason is they never measure up when compared to you."

It was Ash's turn to be stunned, "You mean?" Ash left the question hanging in the air. "Yup," Daniel said as he leant forward and gave Ash a kiss on the mouth. Ash felt like time had stood still, and all she could say was, "James."

Breaking the kiss, Daniel smiled at her, "How about we go and have some breakfast? Oh and Ash, my name's Daniel."

Paula knocked on the girl's door. "Come in," Steph said. Paula opened the door to see both girls peeping through the net curtains out to where Daniel and Ash were sitting.

"What are you doing?" Paula demanded.

"Shhh," they hissed back, "I think Daniel's going to kiss Ash…" Gina said quietly.

"Don't be silly," Paula said peeking out at the same time, as her words trailed off as right at that moment Daniel kissed Ash.

"Oh," all three of them said in unison. "Right, now we've have seen them kiss, get away from that window, or you might just scare your brother back to Dr Kirkland's," Paula ordered.

It was the small things Paula realised. The simple act of making breakfast for her son. Hearing her three children joking and teasing each other. Seeing the looks of first love on her son's face. Each moment was causing tears to run down Paula's face. "Oh no, Moms leaking again." become the catch call from each of the kids joking. At each bit of ribbing, Paula would smile, and turn away to wipe the tears with a handkerchief Dennis had handed her; she was the happiest she could ever remember being.

Ash looked at her watch and groaned. "This is great fun and all guys, but I think it is too late to hit the library today. Daniel, we better get going or your father…" Ash paused, "sorry I mean Dr Kirkland, will get suspicious." Daniel got up and gave Paula a hug.

"Hey, I will drop you two back near your house," Dennis said grabbing his keys. "Hey thanks, Dad." Daniel looked over at Paula with a raised eyebrow and paused. "Get out of here you lout, I'm over crying over you today," Paula remarked dabbing the handkerchief to her eyes while smiling. Dennis dropped Ash and Daniel off one street over so no one would notice.

As they walked back, Daniel slid his hand into Ash's. "Smooth move," Ash stated as she grinned up at him. They broke apart at Ash's house, and Daniel continued to his. "I have to find some evidence," Daniel told himself. He needed it just as much as Paula. Dr Kirkland watched James arrive home with growing anger from the master bedroom window. The boy has another thing coming if he thinks he had keep secrets from me, Kirkland raged in his head.

36

Daniel opened the front door and went in. "Where do you think you're going?" Dr Kirkland stood in the doorway to the formal lounge; his hands were crossed, and he looked less than impressed. "I want a word with you." James had an uneasy feeling that was rapidly making him sick to the stomach. "I know your secret James, and I am thoroughly disappointed in you. "Sneaking around behind my back like I would never find out. How stupid do you think I am?" Dr Kirkland raged.

Daniel stood there unsure what to do, should he let fly with the accusations or keep his mouth shut. "Well, what have you got to say for yourself young man, having a relationship with, with that… tramp from down the street." Dr Kirkland stuttered with anger. For Daniel the relief was almost too much, he quickly fought to control his expression least the smallest hint of relief show and give the game away. The relief that the big secret had not be discovered was quickly replaced with anger. Dr Kirkland had no right to speak about Ash in that way.

Daniel decided that attack was the best defence. "I love her and don't you ever talk about her like that again!" Daniel moved towards his father as he almost spat out the words. Seeing shock register on Dr Kirkland's face was almost too much for Daniel, he was trying not to burst out laughing. Turning on his heal, he stomped off upstairs, to his room. Lying on his bed, Daniel felt elated. For the first time, he had stood up to his father. Well, ok, not his birth father, but the feeling was great none the less.

Ben was sitting on the couch when Ash walked back into the house. "Hey sport, hows it going?" he asked cheerfully. Ash moved around the side of the sofa and crashed onto it laying her head on her father's lap.

Ash looked up at her father, "Complicated," she replied.

Ben looked down at his daughter, "Ok, so how was the prize giving," he asked.

Ash sat up, "That's where it gets complicated," Ash paused, "Dad, some people are real dicks." Ash said laying her head back in her father's lap. Ben didn't say anything; he knew that Ash would share more when she needed to. Ash played with a hole in Ben's jeans, "James told me he loves me today.," Ash had almost said, Daniel. "And you said?" Ben enquired. "I said I love him too." Replied Ash. Ben looked down at Ash, "So is now the time I invite a certain young James Kirkland over for a chat while I clean some of my guns and buy a new shovel?" Ben asked.

Ash looked up at her father, "Oh, like you shoot fast enough to hit my boyfriend," Ash teased.

"So he's your boyfriend then?" Ben asked with raised an eyebrow. "You ok with this Dad?" Ash asked.

Ben looked down at his beautiful daughter who was idly making the hole in his knee of his jeans larger. She was in many ways confident beyond her years, but she never seemed to stop worrying about him. Like any father, he would be happy if his daughter became a nun, but he knew Ash carried more maturity than most girls her age. He liked James, at times felt sorry for him having a father like Simon

Kirkland, but he also respected him, and he respected James's choice. His daughter was special and any boy that recognised that was probably ok. "I'm ok sport, guessed you would grow up and have a boyfriend sometime, but I still think I could catch him," Ben replied. "In your dreams Dad, in your dreams," Ash smiled up at her father. Ben smiled back at Ash, "For the record, I am surprised it has taken the champ this long." This comment resulted in a hug.

"I love you Dad." said Ash as she squeezed him just a little harder.

Simon Kirkland was annoyed, firstly he had to admit to himself that he had forgotten to ring the school first thing, the run in with James over dating that tramp and now he had been stuck in surgery for the rest of the day. Three complicated patients had destroyed any chance of following up with the school. Adding to his temper, a call from the Fletchers asking when they could expect delivery of their package and demanding a face to face meeting on Saturday at a cafe they had booked. If they read their damn contract, they would know there can be delays. Kirkland raged in his head. Do they think I just take a baby down off the shelf and unwrap it?

Simon looked down at his diary to confirm nothing else was booked. Taking a yellow pen, he wrote in the Saturday section; Fletchers - Carl and Debra, 2:30 pm Riverside Cafe. Getting up from his desk Simon headed off to bed; it had been a long and frustrating day.

37

Daniel sat quietly listening for the sound of Dr Kirkland's footsteps on the upstairs landing. It was 11:02 pm on his bedside clock when he heard the distinctive squeak of the loose board near his father's room. Daniel waited another twenty minutes until he heard the sound of snoring before slipping out the door.

The landing was not the only part of the house that contained loose boards; there were three more on the staircase. These posed no problem to Daniel as carefully negotiated each hazard in turn. Like most kids, Daniel had wanted to be a spy when he was young, so sneaking around the house was something he had practised in his formative years. On reaching the bottom of the stairs, Daniel headed straight to Dr Kirkland's study.

Taking out a flashlight Daniel surveyed the room. He must hide some evidence somewhere. Daniel thought to himself, But where? The flashlight beam washed over the built-in wooden bookshelves filled with old books that were more for looks than reading. No, not there. Daniel knew. He had played down here many times as a child. Like many children, he had imagined how great it would be to find a secret room behind a bookcase. He had searched for a secret opening in the past to no effect. He continued to play the light across the walls until it came to rest on the family portrait on the wall behind the desk. Daniel now hated that picture and all it represented. Wait a minute, Daniel thought to himself, That was hanging crooked the other way last week.

Moving closer Daniel shone the light behind the painting. "Bingo," there was something hidden behind. Daniel carefully checked all around the painting for any hidden alarm trigger but could find none. Carefully lifting the picture from the wall Daniel could see a safe hidden behind. It was one of those combination dial safes that you see in the movies. Daniel returned the painting back into place ensuring it was tilted just the same amount as before. Daniel moved to the desk and noticed Dr Kirkland's diary laying open to Saturday. There were plenty of entries in blue and black pen on other days but the one inscribed for Saturday was in yellow ink.

What a strange colour to use, Daniel thought to himself; it made it hard to see as it was close in colour to the pages. Flicking back through this year's pages he found very few yellow pen entries, only three. One thing Daniel knew is that his former father was a creature of habit. The yellow entries were no random event. But what is the connection? He asked himself. Looking back at the yellow headings, Daniel noticed that they all occurred after Dr Kirkland's regular working hours. Thumbing back to the Friday of the Laker awards Daniel could see that event but it was in blue ink.

Whatever these meetings were, they were not regular work or life. Dr Kirkland was having a meeting with a couple at 2:30 pm. We just might need to go and see what happens. Daniel thought. Making his way back out of the study, he carefully navigated back to his room. The girls are going to love this. He thought to himself as he lay back down to sleep.

38

They had decided it was safer if the twins and Daniel were not seen together too often. So the next day Ash and Daniel sat together at lunch by themselves. News of their relationship had moved through the school like wildfire, and Daniel's groupies had left to sit at other tables realising that Daniel was off the menu. The kids had decided that messages from Daniel would be routed through Ash who would then deliver them to Gina or Steph. This way few people would see the triplets together, making it much less likely that people would start to talk. If anyone had noticed the change from the four of them hanging out, they would have put it down to Ash and Daniels new relationship.

"So we have a safe, any idea of the combination?" Ash asked after Daniel told her of his night-time raid.

"No idea, but I know the brand and model, it's a Gardall Heavy Duty. I have been racking my brains all morning trying to guess what the number is," he replied.

Ash drummed her figures on the table, "Ok so we don't know the combination, yet. The most pressing thing is this meeting, what do we know about the Fletchers?" she asked.

Daniel pulled out a few sheets of paper, "I did a google search on them this morning. Husband and wife no kids. He owns some big high-tech company that makes chips for cellphones." Turning a page, he continued, "Forbes puts his personal wealth at over $48 million. Oh and I have a couple of photos of the Fletchers here." he finished, showing Ash the last page in his pile.

"That's some serious money, are they from around here?" she asked. "Nope Silicon Valley. A bit of a long way to come for coffee," Daniel announced.

Ash got up from her seat, "I better get this to Gina and Steph asap, walk you home after school?" she asked.

"I guess," Daniel grinned and shrugged earning him a punch in the arm.

Ash moved across the lunch room, and as she neared the twins, she dropped her bag. Items spilt out onto the floor. Collecting them up Ash looked up to see if Gina or Steph had got the message. Gina ever so slightly tilted her head to the left. Yup, message received. Ash thought and headed off to the meeting place behind the new library. Gina and Steph gave it a few minutes before they made their exit. They didn't want to make it look like they were following Ash out. Behind the new library was a cold and damp area where even necking couples avoided as it really was unpleasant there. Steph was the first to speak, "So what's news?" she asked. "Daniel searched Dr Kirkland's study last night after he had gone to sleep," Ash explained. "He found a safe and an entry in Dr Kirkland's diary."

Gina looked hopeful, "Do we know what the number is for the safe?" she asked.

"No, not yet. Daniel says it's one of those dial based combo locks you see in the movies," Ash replied.

"What about the entry in the diary, any leads there?" Gina enquired.

Ash explained about the Fletcher's and the meeting on Saturday while handing them the printed sheets from Daniel.

"So where's this cafe? Don't suppose we could stake it out?" Steph asked.

Ash thought for a moment, "The Riverside Cafe is right on the bank of the Hesp River, you can sit outside on this floating marina thing, there are reeds on the other side of the river… How big is your lens for your camera?" she asked Gina.

Gina grinned, "The biggest I have got is a 50-500mm Sigma zoom," she replied.

Ash nodded, "That should be big enough. We won't be able to hear what they say but we can at least snap some pics," she stated. "Sounds good. Let's give it a try. You sure no one will see us from the other side?" Steph asked.

"Nah, heaps of cover over that side of the river," Ash explained. "So what do we tell the boy, he would give the game up if Kirkland sees him?" Gina asked.

Ash Groaned, "He ain't gonna want to sit this one out, but he would stuff it up royally if he's spotted."

Gina and Steph nodded. Ash sighed, "Ok, I'll break the news to him, but he's not going to take this well," Ash wondered off in search of Daniel.

39

Simon had finally remembered to call the school. He had got through to Principal Jones straight away. "Hello Dr Kirkland," Ms Jones answered, "How may I help you today?" she asked.

"Ms Jones, I was wondering if you could give me a hand? I met the mother of the two other Laker prize winners, and for the life of me, I can't remember her name or the name of the girls. I wanted to send them a congratulations card, and I would feel very embarrassed to get their names wrong," Simon lied.

"Oh that's no problem Dr Kirkland, I am terrible with names myself, let me just get their file," Ms Jones returned half a minute later. "Ok here is it is, the mother's name is, oh that's unusual, it only has an initial and surname, P. Farley, but I do have the girls names, Steph and Gina," she advised.

"Thank you, Ms Jones. The other night you thought Mrs Farley's name was Philippa, do you think that might be correct?" Dr Kirkland asked.

"Oh, yes that must be it, but your wrong about one thing Dr Kirkland, the girl's mother isn't married I am certain she is Miss Farley, not Mrs," stated Ms Jones.

Simon felt a wave of relief; this must be one of those weird coincidences in life. "Thank you, Ms Jones, you have been very helpful, goodbye," he said hanging up. Simon double clicked on Internet Explorer and typed in a search on 'P Farley and Gina and Steph Farley'. The result came back with over four hundred results. A quick scan revealed hits from all over the US. There were Paula's, Philippa's, Patricia's and many others not beginning with the letter P. Yes thought Simon to himself. Just like he thought. There were so many people in the US that name combinations like this were not uncommon. But the nagging feeling that he had met her before remained. Picking up the phone, Simon made a call. "Derrick Pullman Investigations," came the answer.

"Mr Pullman, Simon Kirkland here, I would like to have a meeting if you are available?" Kirkland asked.

"Certainly Dr Kirkland, I am tied up at present until Monday next week, I hope that is not too long a wait?" Pullman asked.

Simon looked at his diary, "Monday week would work at 6 pm. Old Coach Road Diner?" Simon enquired about the location of the meeting.

"That will be fine, I will see you then," Pullman rang off.

Derrick Pullman clicked into his calendar on his laptop and entered the meeting time and date. Derrick chuckled to himself. Bet the old man never eats there if he doesn't have to, he thought, Nowhere near fancy enough for the posh, stuck up, Dr Kirkland. Derrick might not think highly of Simon Kirkland, but he did pay very well. The work Derrick Pullman did for Simon Kirkland was not in his regular line of work. No, these jobs were off the books and often very illegal. The work was varied, sometimes it was research on clients to ensure Kirkland was not setup, other times it was to scare employees and remind them to keep their mouths shut. All high risk but high reward as well.

Derrick closed his computer as he wondered what Dr Kirkland had in store for him this time.

40

Ash couldn't find Daniel, so the news had to wait until their walk home. Daniel was not impressed. "So I bring you the info, and now you three get to go and risk getting spotted?" Daniel exclaimed.

Ash needed to be tactful, "That's the point, if we get spotted then it is easier to explain. If you get spotted then the game is up," she replied.

Daniel huffed out an exasperated sound, "So I get to sit at home like a frightened old lady while my girlfriend and my sisters take all the risk?" he said, clearly annoyed.

Ash had the benefit of thinking about this already, "No we need you to research that safe, so we know how many numbers it needs to open. And I had an idea about that as well. We need a photo of the study so we can look for anything obvious that might be the code," she replied.

"And just how am I going to get a photo?" Daniel asked.

Ash grinned, "That part is simple. Just tell Dr Kirkland you need a photo for a journalism project for school. Tell him that you have to photograph someone important. He'll fall for that like heroin addict goes for crack," Ash smiled at her example of how fond of attention Dr Kirkland was.

Daniel had to agree that plan was brilliant. A photo would give them all time to study it for any clues for the combination for the safe. But he was still nervous about the girls going on the stakeout, "Ok, but you let me know as soon as you are back. I have lost too many years already without putting the next ones in jeopardy," he replied. Ash was touched by his concern for her and his family, "Deal, now I better get going and finish the planning with the twins," she replied, giving Daniel a kiss on the cheek.

Daniel arrived home and went and found his camera and turned it on. "Yes!" Daniel exclaimed, it still had some charge. Grabbing the camera, Daniel headed off downstairs in search of Dr Kirkland. He was not surprised to find his former father at his desk in his study. Daniel knocked on the door.

"Ah, James comes in," Dr Kirkland answered. "What can I do for you?" he asked, barely looking up from his work as Daniel entered.

Daniel put on his most polite voice, "Excuse me, Sir; we have been given a journalism assignment for school. They have told us to take a photo of someone important, and I wondered if you would let me photograph you," Daniel asked.

"Well," Dr Kirkland was already puffing up, thinking his son considered him important, "I guess that would be okay. Where would you like to take the photo?" Dr Kirkland replied.

Daniel raised the camera, "How about here, in your study?" he asked. "I could take them now if you have the time. It should look like you are working, sort of a photojournalism thing," he said continuing the ruse.

Dr Kirkland nodded, "All right James, now would be good, it would give us some time to talk as well," he replied.

Daniel's heart rate shot up. "Ok, um I need to take a few photos and then I have to submit the best one," Daniel explained taking the lens cap off the camera and turning on the flash.

Dr Kirkland sat behind his desk as Daniel took plenty of photos from lots of different angles. Daniel was pretty sure that he had covered every square inch of the study. Now, only time and some hard searching would tell. As Daniel was taking the photos, Dr Kirkland was asking him about the new family, the Farley's.

"What do you know about the new girls at school, the twins, the ones who also won the maths prize?" he asked.

"Um, not much actually, I am paired up with one of them, Gina, for Science," Daniel thought it best to keep the answers as close to the truth as possible. Thinking on his feet, Daniel came up with an idea. "They are both pretty snooty, so Ash and I don't have much to do with them," he lied.

"What about the mother, what is she like?" Dr Kirkland asked.

Daniel focused on getting the story right, "I don't know her either. I had just met her the night of the library opening, the twins introduced me," he replied, "Why are you interested in them?" he asked casually.

"Oh, I thought I recognised the mother and I couldn't place her. It will come to me at some point, I'm sure," Dr Kirkland replied. Daniel lowered his camera, "Ok, well thank you, sir; I think I have what I need." Daniel figured it was time to lay it on thick, "You know this is probably going to be the easiest assignment ever, no one else in my class has someone quite as important as you at home that they can simply take photos of," he stated. Seeing the look on Dr Kirkland's face was all the confirmation he needed. Puffed up twit. Daniel thought to himself as he left the room, but he had the growing fear that Dr Kirkland would remember who his mother was, and if that happened all hell would break loose.

41

Gina, Steph and Ash were gearing up for their spying over at Ash's. One of the problems was ensuring that they were not spotted in the reeds at the side of the river. Gina and Steph didn't have any clothes that would work, so they raided Ash's house for anything that would help them hide. They ended up all choosing black jeans and dark tops out of Ash's closet covered by some old hunting jackets of Ben's. "We are going to have to take this stuff in a bag." Gina pointed out, "We would look rather odd walking down to the river looking like this." Ash found two backpacks and they loaded all the clothes in, while Gina checked the camera gear over.

While they were packing, there was a knock at the door, and Daniel walked in. "Hey," he said walking in, giving Ash a kiss, "great you're all here. I got the photos and-and some detail about the safe."

Steph looked over at Ash and Daniel, "You two need a room?" she joked.

Ash blushed while Daniel had a grin on his face. "Feel you're missing out Steph. Need a kiss from your brother?" Daniel said puckered up and moving towards her.

"Eew yuck, no, get away that's gross," Steph exclaimed climbing up on Ash's bed to avoid Daniel. The action caused all four of them to burst into laughter.

Once the laughter had subsided, Daniel told them about the questioning from Dr Kirkland.

Steph looked concerned, "This could be a major problem, do you think he will join the dots?" she asked.

"I'm not sure, could he confirm your names somehow?" Daniel asked.

Ash sat on her bed thinking, "What if he calls the school, they have all your details don't they?" she asked.

Gina thought about this for a moment, "Mom registered us under Farley, not her maiden name, that might help muddy the waters. Also, Stephanie was registered as Steph," Gina replied.

Ash looked at each of them, "Pretty thin disguise; it won't take much checking on Google to put Farley and Johnson together. One plus one will add up to two pretty quickly," she pointed out.

Steph was grinning, "What's so funny?" Ash asked.

"One plus one," Steph paused, "Don't you mean two plus one?" she replied laughing.

Daniel punched her in the arm, "Git!" he replied, "It should be ok, Dr Kirkland is hopeless on a computer, so I doubt he will find anything. Even if he did, I guess there is not much we can do about it anyway. If he does put the details together, then I bolt as we planned. Do you want to look at the photos?" he asked holding out a USB pen drive.

"Toss it here," Ash replied.

Ash downloaded all the photos onto her laptop, and the four of them gathered around the small screen. "This is going to be impossible on this tiny screen," Daniel pointed out.

Ash looked at Daniel, "What are you saying Daniel? You know size is not everything!" Gina and Steph burst out laughing again, as it was Daniel's turn to blush. Ash unplugged her laptop, "Come on, we'll use Dad's TV downstairs." They all trooped downstairs, and Ash connected her laptop up to the 43" Plasma.

"Nice tv!" Steph commented.

"Dad likes his toys," Ben said coming into the room.

"Oh, hi dad didn't know you were home," Ash replied.

"Quiet day, the boss let me go early due to all the nights this week. What are you doing? Movie?" Ben asked, casually.

Ash shook her head, "No, it's an assignment. We have been given this mystery to solve. We know there is a hidden safe in the room, and we now need to find the combination," she lied to the astonishment of the others.

"Cool, let me know if you need some professional help finding the clues," Ben offered, joking as he left the room.

"Ash!" Gina whispered. "You could have got us caught!"

"Don't panic, dad might be useful to us yet if we can't find a clue," Ash replied.

Ash brought up the photos that Daniel had taken. There were twenty-two images, but only one had Dr Kirkland in it. Daniel had skilfully managed to focus on just about every inch of the room while avoiding Dr Kirkland. Ash quickly deleted the image with Dr Kirkland off her hard drive. "There you go," she exclaimed, "if we need his help, no risk." The others had to agree this was a good move. An hour later they had found 14 different number combinations.

"Daniel, this is so frustrating!" Steph complained. "It could be any one of these, or a combination them!

Ben returned to the room carrying a bowl of crisps and four cans of 7 Up. "Thought you could all do with some fuel. Figured it out yet?" he asked.

Ash grabbed a can and clicked it open. "No, not yet, we have some combinations, but we will have to get them checked," she replied. "This is just an assignment, right? I'm not going to have to visit my daughter behind bars am I?" Ben jokingly asked.

All four kids laughed. "No it's just homework Mr Smith," Daniel replied.

"Ok then," Ben replied. Just as Ben was leaving the room he stopped and turned, "Hey, by the way, why do you keep calling James, Daniel? Is this some game I should know about?"

Ash grabbed Daniel in a hug, "No it's just my unique name for my lover boy," she replied laughing. Ben left the room shaking his head. He could never be sure when Ash was winding him up or being serious.

42

All four of the kids look at one another, and Daniel was the first to voice his thoughts, "Man that was close, fast move, Ash."

Gina slowly exhaled, "We all have to be more careful, but this double name business is doing my head in," she said, voicing the same thoughts the others were having.

"Ok so I have to go, you girls give me a half hour head start. Ok?" Daniel suggested.

"Right, see you Monday," Gina replied. The three girls watched as Daniel headed out the door. "It's killing him being apart from his real family," Ash observed.

"We know, we can feel it, his pain, he's torn. It's not physical; it's emotional, and it's hurting him," Steph replied.

Gina nodded, "I'm just not sure what we can do about it yet. We need that evidence to bring down Kirkland. Until then we're all stuck like this," Gina pointed out.

"How about us all get-together tomorrow night, after the meeting?" Ash asked, "I could tell him we are going out to tea and then to the movies. We could all meet at the motel and just hang. That way he gets to spend time with you guys and Paula," she explained.

"Perfect, and I have another idea, and Mom is just going to die for it," replied Gina. "Come on Steph we need to book it back to the motel."

"Are you going to let me in on what you have planned?" Ash asked. "No time, sorry Ash," Gina said grabbing Steph on the way out the door. "You just make sure you get Daniel there, in time for dinner."

Gina explained the plan on the way back to the motel. By the time they had got there, the two girls were just about exploding with enthusiasm. Gina's idea was to throw Daniel a birthday party, not just one birthday party, but one for each year he had missed out on. "I hope you don't expect me to bake sixteen cakes by tomorrow," Paula exclaimed after hearing the plan.

"No, just one, but it will need to be big," Steph replied. Paula was just as enthusiastic as the twins and within minutes had them in the car off to the mall for supplies. The plan was to try and find foods, games and presents for each of the years Daniel had missed. Paula herded the girls into the car and the shot off into town to find what they needed. In the end, most of the items were found in Walmart and took two trolley loads to get it all to the car. It was when they got back to the car that the obvious flaw in their plan was evident.

"How are we going to get this all in the car?" Paula asked. In the end, they managed by Gina sitting in the front seat while they piled party stuff on top of her. A similar thing had to happen to Steph as well in the back seat. It looked like Walmart had exploded inside the car. Paula was about half a mile from the motel when she noticed the lights and siren of a police car. Pulling over Paula groaned, "Not now, we were almost home," Paula wound down the window as the police officer approached. "Yes, Officer, is something wrong?" Paula asked batting her eyes at the officer as he looked on in amazement.

"Gina, Steph? What is going on?" Ben asked looking at the mostly covered twins with a stunned look on his face.

"Oh, Hi Mr Smith," Gina replied. "We are throwing a party for, um, James," she replied.

"This is some party," Ben said looking through the windows, "and probably not the safest way to transport it all," Ben continued, "How far do you have to go?" he asked.

"Oh only up to the Travel Lodge Motel on Fourth Street, I'm so sorry officer?" indicating she did not know his name.

"Smith, Ben Smith ma'am," Ben added.

"Yes as I was saying, Officer Smith, I'm so sorry, we got carried away," Paula replied.

"Ash is bringing James over tomorrow night," Steph added.

Ben sighed, "Ok, well I guess no 'major' rules have been broken, but please don't try this again. Oh, and ladies, do have fun," Ben waved them on while shaking his head.

The woman in this town are going nuts, he thought to himself.

43

Paula and the girls unloaded the car. "Damn," Paula exclaimed, "How are we going to bake a cake, we don't even have an oven?" The girls all looked at one another, "What about asking Lexi?" Steph asked.

"We can only but ask," Paula replied. They trooped over to the office, "Hey, how are my loveliest and longest customers?" greeted Lexi. "What can I be doing for you today?" she asked.

"Lexi we have a little bit of a problem, we are throwing a party for a friend of the twins and we just realised that we have no way to bake a cake," Paula replied.

"Oh you need to use my oven, you don't need to ask just come and use it anytime," Lexi gushed. "I can give you a hand if you like," she said.

"That would be great, Mom and Steph you go and sort out the games and stuff, Lexi and I will go bang out a cake," Gina offered. "Oh thank you, Lexi, you have got us out of a bind," Paula thanked Lexi. "Gina come and get the ingredients," she instructed.

Lexi's unit was a blast from the past. Full-length shag-pile carpets, built-in furniture, with pink floral curtains, tied back with sashes. Gina felt like she had stepped back in time. Lexi noted the surprised look on her face. "Pretty wild huh? The previous manager had a thing for Elvis, so he tried to recreate the look. Didn't get there," Lexi grinned, "still I guess I should be thankful there's no 'jungle room,'" she laughed. Lexi was a cake making machine, ingredients few into the mixing bowl and before long the mixture was in the oven in the biggest cake tin Gina had ever seen. "Right how about a cup of coffee while we wait?" Lexi asked.

"Sounds great," Gina replied. Lexi set out two cups and boiled the jug. "So tell me how you are settling in? Didn't think you folk would end up staying," she stated.

"Well, Mom thought Greenspan would be good for her business, and it has worked out well. Heaps of lovely antiques here in Texas Mom says," Gina replied.

Lexi stirred some sugar into her coffee, "So who is this friend you are throwing this party for? Don't suppose it's that lovely young man James Kirkland?" Lexi winked at Gina, "quite a hunk, that boy." Gina laughed, "Yes it is James, but no we are not interested in him, not like that anyway. He's going out with another one of our friends, Ash Smith," Gina replied.

Lexi smiled, "Oh, Ben Smith's girl. Strange child, always wearing black. Been like that since her mama died when she was eight. Still Ben's a nice man, real salt and light type that one, lovely just lovely," Lexi gushed.

In no time the smell of freshly baked cake was filling the kitchen. "That smells great," Gina commented.

"Is your momma going to ice it? If she is you just make sure she does it when it's cold," Lexi advised.

"Well I better get this over to Mom, thank you so much, Lexi, I'll bring you over a piece," Gina replied.

"That would be lovely dear, just make sure it's a small one, I can't fit much more cake into this body," Lexi said giving her ample chest a push up while laughing.

Gina carried the cake back over to Paula's room. Outside there was a strange car parked with its trunk open. "Dad!" Exclaimed Gina as she entered with the cake. Dennis was in the middle of an 'I've missed you' embrace with Paula. "Ugh, get a room" Gina exclaimed.

"We have a room; you just barged into it!" Paula replied with a smirk. "Oh wow, that cake looks awesome! Lexi is a saint."

"Is the cake for supper?" Dennis asked hopefully.

"No, and you keep your sticky hands off it Dennis Farley or so help me…" Paula was giving him one of her, 'don't try me' looks. Gina was grinning like a Cheshire cat when Paula turned to her, "And don't you get any ideas either missy, I still remember when you cut the middle out of my birthday cake, stuffed it with paper towels and iced it," Paula ranted. "There will be NO pranking your brother on his birthday! And Stephanie, I know you can hear me, so that goes for you as well!"

"Ok," Steph replied from the other room.

Paula's speech was over. Gina put the cake on the table and quickly exited the room. "I'll just leave you both in peace then," Gina grinned over her shoulder as she closed the door.

"Wise-arses, all of them. They must take after you," Paula said pointing at Dennis. "Come here," Dennis said, "let's figure out where we were before we were interrupted."

44

Dr Kirkland was going out for the evening, and this gave Daniel the perfect time to try some of the numbers they had found. He waited half an hour after Dr Kirkland had left before going downstairs to his study. This time Daniel afforded himself the luxury of turning the lights on. Daniel carefully noted the angle of the family portrait and then gently removed it from it the wall. Taking out a piece of the notepad with the numbers on it, he began the laborious process of trying each one.

Ash had suggested trying some obvious numbers like birthdays, anniversaries, social security numbers, even the numbers of books on each shelf of the bookshelves. Given all those options Daniel had only just returned the family portrait to the wall and switched out the lights when he heard Dr Kirkland's car return. Back in his room, Daniel looked at his watch, damn, two and three-quarter hours, and nothing to show for it. He thought to himself in frustration.

It was going to be a big day for Ash, Gina and Steph. There were still party things for the twins to organise, and then they needed to meet Ash at the river at 2:00 pm. During the night Ash had thought of a plan that would allow them to listen in to Dr Kirkland's meeting. At 10 am Ash made a phone call. "Hello, River Side Cafe, how may I help you?" Answered the phone.

"Yes hello, we have a reservation for 2:30 pm today under Fletcher. We were wondering if we could have the table closest to the riverside?" Ash asked.

"Just a moment while I check that table is free." Came the response down the phone. Ash waited while the man on the phone checked the details. "That's no problem the table is free, and I have booked it for your party at 2:30 pm. Will that be all?" he asked.

Ash grinned to herself, "Yes thank you, that's wonderful, we will see you at 2:30 pm, thank you for your help," Ash ended the call. Right, that's one job done now for the next part, Ash thought to herself. Grabbing a jacket, she headed downstairs to look for her Dad. Ben was reading the morning paper at the table. "Dad, any chance you could drop me over to the Gina and Steph's in a couple of minutes? I need to help them with part of that assignment again," Ash asked. "Sure thing, I was thinking of heading into town anyway to get some bread and milk. You want to go now?" Ben asked.

"That would be great," Ash replied, as Ben stood up and went to get his keys and a jacket.

"So I pulled up this weird car yesterday filled with party supplies. When I say filled up I mean there were two girls buried under all the stuff and the mother couldn't even see out of the back window," Ben explained, while pulling into the Motel car park.

"Weird, what did you say to the woman and the girls?" Ash asked. "You can ask them yourself when you see them," Ben said pulling up in front of the Farley's. "You want me to come and pick you up later?" he asked.

Ash shook her head, "No I'll make my own way home, thanks for the lift," Ash blew her dad a kiss and gave him a wave as she hopped out of the car. As Ash knocked on

Paula's door, she wondered what on earth the Farley's needed with a heap of… her thoughts trailed off as Dennis opened the door, revealing the scene within. The room was fully decorated for a child's birthday party. There were streamers, a happy birthday banner, plastic cups set out on the table and a huge crazy looking cake. Ash walked in and took a closer look at the cake; it looked crazy. The cake had been iced, but what made it look weird was the sixteen different number candles stuck in the top, 1 through to 16.

"The girls thought Daniel could do with cheering up," Dennis explained. "Gina came up with this crazy idea of throwing him a birthday party; then Steph said we should throw him one for every year we have missed."

Ash starting laughing so hard she just about wet herself. "Oh, he is just going to die when he gets a load of this," she said.

45

Paula came through from the bedroom. "Oh, hi Ash," Paula said giving Ash a big hug. "Welcome to the land of Crazy! Girls Ash is here." Paula called out to the connected room.

Gina and Steph came in. "What do you think? Steph asked.

"I think you guys have hit it out of the park; he's going to freak. Oh, but just one small thing, you're all crazy!" Ash grinned. "I have got some good news. I have figured out a way to allow us to hear what is said at the Fletcher's meeting." Ash went on to explain. "I rang the Cafe and pretended to be the Fletcher's and asked if we could sit at the closest table to the river."

"That's great Ash, but you will never hear them all the way across the water," Paula pointed out.

"Ah but that is where you and Mr Farley come in. You need to go down there just before the Fletcher's and try to get that table. If you can get it then all we need to do is tape my phone under the table with some duct tape," Ash explained.

"But what if someone calls you, they will hear it ring?" Dennis asked.

"But it won't ring because you will have called Paula's phone just before you stick it up. When the Fletcher's are gone, someone goes back and retrieves the phone," Ash replied.

"So while they have their meeting, you and the girls will be on the other side of the river taking photo's and listening in?" Paula stated, nodding. "How can we ensure they sit at that table? This will only work if they sit at that exact table," Paula thought out loud.

"There is only one table out of this little jetty that sticks out into the river. All the other tables on the shore are close together. I thought if they are going to talk about something sensitive it would have to be at that table," Ash replied.

"Way to go, Ash, it's a fantastic idea!" Gina's praise resulted in a grin on Ash's face.

Paula and Dennis got ready quickly if the plan was to succeed they needed to ensure they got the table early and only give it up at the last minute before the Fletcher meeting. Dennis and Paula drove the girls to the opposite side of the river. Gina, Steph and Ash looked like commandos, dressed in black jeans and dark brown hunting jackets. The twins wore beanies to disguise their long brown hair. For the girls, this would be a long wait until 2:30 pm. They moved down into the reeds at the edge of the river, found a good spot and got the camera and mobile phone ready.

Dennis and Paula pulled into the car park outside the River Side Cafe, and they both got out and headed for the entrance. "Hello, a table for two?" A cheerful waiter asked.

"Oh yes please, but we do have a special request," replied Paula. "Certainly, how may we help?" he replied.

"Well my husband and I, well we had our first date here. We sat out on the river, it was so romantic, I, we wondered if we could have that table again?" Paula lied, while Dennis pulled her into a hug.

"Let me see if it is booked," Replied the waiter smiling.

"Smooth, honey, very smooth." Dennis quietly commented as the waiter went off to check. Paula grinned.

The waiter returned quickly, "We have a booking at 2:30 pm, but I could offer you the table until 2, if that is ok, I would give you longer, but we will need to ensure it is cleaned and set up for the next booking," he advised.

"Oh that is plenty of time, isn't it honey?" Paula gushed.

"Yes, thank you, sir," Dennis replied slipping the waiter a twenty.

The waiter guided Dennis and Paula down to the table by the river and produced two menus. After advising them of the specials he quietly slipped away giving them some time to decide and make a quick call.

"They're there!" Gina announced. Gina could see Paula, Dennis and a man she assumed was the waiter coming down the jetty to the table. The waiter continued to speak to them for a few minutes and then left.

The phone in Steph's hand began to ring. "Hello, Steph it's Mom. Are you in position?" Paula asked down the line.

"Hi Mom, yes we think we have a good spot, we can see you clearly. Can you see us?" Steph asked. Paula spoke to Dennis, and within moments they were both searching along the river bank for any sign of the three girls.

"Nope can't see any sign of you," Paula replied after a minute or so. "Have them move a little bit," Steph could hear Dennis say in the background.

"Did you hear your father?" Paula asked. "Yes, hold on," Steph replied.

"They want us to move a bit to see if we show up," Steph announced to the others. All three moved about a bit, stretching and changing positions, but not making any sudden movements. Steph settled back into her spot, "Could you see any of that?" She asked. Paula and Dennis had been searching the bank for any sign, "No honey, looks like you have a good spot." Paula replied.

"Mum, don't forget to mute the phone before you call us just in case," Steph advised.

"Ok, will do, got to go, the waiter is coming," Paula hung up.

Dennis was doing an excellent job of reviewing the menu and when the waiter asked if they were ready to order he replied, "Yes, please I will have the Eggs Benedict, on whole wheat toast with extra crispy bacon. What would you like my dear?" Paula was amazed, Dennis was unflappable, here they were on a stakeout, and he was ordering a huge meal from the all-day breakfast menu. "Um," Paula was stalling for time as she scanned the menu, "Perhaps the grilled Bagel with Three Cheeses, Tomato and Chorizo Sausages," She asked. "Excellent choices, may I bring you some coffee as well?" The waiter asked.

"Yes, that would be good, Cappuccino for me and a long black for my wife," Dennis replied.

The waiter nodded noting down the order and left leaving Dennis and Paula to themselves. Paula waited until the waiter was out of earshot. "How can you eat a meal like that at a time like this? I am so nervous that I have butterflies in my stomach," Paula exclaimed. "Well we are here, the food looks good; I am hungry, and we are going to have to wait awhile. Add to that the beautiful woman sitting at the table with me and I think I have a great reason to eat a meal at a time like this," Dennis grinned at his wife.

Paula laughed, Yup, her laid-back unflappable man, her fantastic, wonderful, unflappable man. She thought to herself. How could she ever live without him?

Paula had to admit that, after her butterflies had been settled, the food and company was quite good. Although winter, it was a sunny day with no wind, so they were quite comfortable sitting out on the river. Paula glanced at her watch, 1:45 pm. "Dennis it's time." Paula quietly said. Dennis pulled out a short length of duct tape while Paula dialled the girls. "Can you hear us?" she asked.

"Yes, loud and clear," Came the reply. Paula handed Dennis the phone which he attached to the strip of duct tape. Dennis took Paula's hand and bringing it up to his mouth gave it a kiss. At the same time, with his left hand, Dennis slipped the phone under the table and smoothed the tape in place. It was a slick move, to the casual observer it looked like two lovers sharing a moment.

The waiter noticed the kiss and waited a moment longer before bringing them the bill. "I hope everything meets your expectations?" he asked as he offered Dennis the bill.

Paula nodded, "Yes thank you. It was so special getting to sit here again," she replied, squeezing Dennis's hand. Dennis extracted the amount for the bill and a generous tip from his wallet and paid the waiter.

"Many thanks, sir, please enjoy the rest of your day." The waiter moved off. Paula and Dennis stood and had one last look at the other side of the river then walked back up the jetty and out to Paula's car.

46

Simon was not in a good mood. He had already given James a lecture about his recovery taking too long and this meeting with the Fletchers was just another annoyance he could do without. He sat in his car at the lights waiting impatiently for it to go green. The light must be about to change as a small red compact was slowing up to stop that had been heading in the other direction. Simon looked at the driver, a beautiful woman who looked back at him. It's that Farley woman! Simon thought.

The look Paula gave Simon strange, he could not pin it down. One moment she looked angry and the next victorious. Simon just knew at that moment he had seen her somewhere before. He could not place it, but the nagging feeling at the back of his mind was growing into a hard knot of fear. Someone honked for Simon to go, How long have I been sitting here? He asked himself turning past the little red car. Simon glanced at the clock on the dash of his 7 series BMW. 2:04 pm, Good he thought, better to be the first to arrive. Simon needed to get his head into the game.

Dennis was sitting in the passenger seat. He watched Paula's hands grip the steering wheel, and her knuckles go white. His gaze followed hers to the fancy-looking silver BMW stopped at the lights on the left. A man was sitting in the driver's seat looking right back at Paula. The sound of a honking horn brought Dennis back, and the driver of the BMW passed them heading in the direction of the Cafe. "That was him, wasn't it?" Dennis asked.

Paula nodded slowly, "Yes, that son of a bitch is going to burn!" she hissed. A few moments passed then the light turned green. Paula drove off towards the other side of the river where they were going to wait for the girls. Dennis looked at Paula; I would not want to be in Simon Kirkland's shoes when she has her revenge. He thought to himself.

Simon pulled up to the cafe and got out of his car. Finding a waiter he enquired about the booking for the table. "Yes sir, we have reserved the table by the water as requested," replied the waiter. "We are just setting it up now, would you like to wait in the bar while we get it sorted?"

Simon was not really in a waiting frame of mind. Glancing at his watch, he realised that he was still quite early. "Yes I suppose I will have to if the table is not ready," he replied rudely.

The waiter guided Kirkland to the bar and then moved off to finish the table preparations. Taking a bottle of cleaning spray and cloth, the waiter headed off to clean the table. Gina watched him through the big Sigma zoom lens attached to her Canon as he approached the table. Suddenly the waiter lifted one side of the table and gave it a small shake to remove the crumbs from Dennis and Paula's meals. Gina froze, she could clearly see the silver tape holding the phone in place.

"What's that noise?" Steph asked.

"The waiter is tilting the table to wipe away the crumbs. I can see the phone!" Gina replied, her eye still glued to the viewfinder.

"Has he seen it?" Ash asked urgently.

"I'm not sure; he's lowering the table back now. Oh, crap he just dropped something, and he's bending down," Gina relayed to the others.

The waiter bent over to pick up a napkin that had fallen. Suddenly he heard a loud noise across the river as over two dozen waterfowl flew up into the air. Ash had seized the moment and averting the disaster grabbed a hand full of stones and threw them over into an area just up river from their hiding spot. She had hoped it would make enough of a distraction, but she could never have predicted the existence of the waterfowl nesting only a ten feet ahead of them. Scooping up the napkin the waiter watched as the birds soared into the air.

Gina let out a sigh of relief, "He didn't see it. Well done Ash." The girls continued to sit and wait. "It must be soon," Steph started looking at her watch.

"Shhh," Gina said, "someone's coming."

47

Simon walked out on to the jetty and sat down. Glancing at his watch, he noted it was only 2:25 pm. He hated waiting. Seeing movement out of the corner of his eye Simon turned back towards the cafe. A couple in their late thirties were walking down the jetty towards him. The man, Carl Fletcher, Simon recognised from photos in the Wall Street Journal. Fletcher was a tall man with sandy brown hair. Like many in the rapidly expanding tech industry, Carl Fletcher was a high school dropout who seemed more at home in jeans and a polo shirt than a formal suit.

Simon immediately felt overdressed, further adding to his annoyance. Debra Fletcher was nothing special to look at, just a plain Jane, was Simons' first thought. Dressed in an Amani blazer over tight jeans she just looked like she was trying too hard to look rich. They were rich, however, much richer than Simon, and that annoyed him even more.

Gina focused in on the two newcomers and took half a dozen close-up shots. She then pulled back the zoom and got three excellent shots of Dr Kirkland shaking both Carl and Debra's hands. The sound was coming in pretty good over the mobile phone; the girls could clearly hear the greetings. "Dr Kirkland, this is my wife Debra," Carl was heard saying.

"Hello Debra, it is nice to meet you finally," Kirkland replied.

"Shall we order some coffee before getting down to business?" Carl asked.

"Yes that would be good," replied Kirkland.

Simon waved the waiter over. "How may I assist you sir?" the waiter asked.

"We would like to order some coffee," Kirkland replied. "Certainly sir what would you like?"

"I will have a Soy Late," replied Debra.

"And I will have an Expresso," Carl added.

"A short black," Kirkland replied.

"Excellent, I will be back with your drinks in a few minutes." The waiter returned to the cafe building to prepare their drinks.

The coffee took five minutes to arrive and while they waited the Fletcher's and Dr Kirkland mostly spoke about the weather, and the flight down from Silicon Valley in the Fletcher's personal jet a Cessna Citation III. After the coffee arrived the conversation switched to the real business at hand. Gina had changed from still photos to video and the mobile phone was giving them pretty good sound. "So Dr Kirkland, when can we expect our delivery?" Carl asked.

"I would expect within the next seven or eight months at the outside," Simon replied. "The major issue is that we need to wait until I have a patient carrying multiples, twins or more. I have an appointment next week that might fit that bill."

"Why should it matter if it is one or more?" Debra asked.

"Well the mothers ask fewer questions if they get to go home with at least one bundle of joy," Kirkland explained getting annoyed at the woman's question.

"But we have paid you a considerable deposit to get us a baby Mr Kirkland, and you have not delivered," Mrs Fletcher's voice had risen.

"Mrs Fletcher, you need to lower your voice, what we are discussing here is not legal, it is kidnapping! A crime that is a felony in all fifty-two states. I work the way I do to minimise the risk, not only to me but also my clients," Kirkland explained, looking at both the Fletchers in turn.

"But we have not done anything wrong, we have just paid you for a service," Debra replied. "None of this could stick to us."

Carl put his hand on his wife's, "Darling I think it best that we let Dr Kirkland do it his way. We can't risk it going wrong." Debra slumped back into her seat; it was clear that she was not going to get her way.

"I think we are done here, Carl," she promptly stood up and walked back towards the cafe.

"I'm so sorry Dr Kirkland," Carl said standing, "Debra is desperate for a child. We will wait for you to contact us about the baby when it is available. I will talk to her and make sure she understands." Carl shook Simon's hand and headed off to find his wife. After about five minutes Simon finished his coffee and stood up to head back to his car. As he was passing the reception desk, the waiter called out to him, "Excuse me, sir, the bill?" Simon wandered over and took a look, "Typical," he grunted, the Fletchers had left without paying.

The girls waited ten minutes after Dr Kirkland before they moved back up the river bank. They were still in a euphoric mood when they reached the car with Paula and Dennis dozing in the front seat. "Well?" Paula asked.

Steph produced a small dictaphone from her pocket. "Got it all, he even explained why he targets woman carrying multiples," Steph replied.

"So what now?" asked Ash. "Well, first things first we need to go and get your mobile phone back. Then we will drop you back at your place, and you can get showered and cleaned up for the party." Paula replied.

"Are we not going to do anything about the video and recording today?" Gina asked.

"No today is party day, we have done plenty of work today; now it is time to party!" Paula announced with a huge smile on her face. "Dr Kirkland's time will come soon," she announced.

Dennis drove them back to the Cafe and Paula hopped out. Heading back into the cafe she bumped into their waiter. "Oh hello, back already?" he asked smiling. Paula battered her eyes, "I'm so sorry I seem to have forgotten my mobile phone, I will just go and get it." Paula said smiling. The waiter followed her out to the table where Paula tilted the table up and peeled the phone from under the table. The waiter just looked at her with eyes wide as saucers. Paula stopped next to him and pressed another $20 note into his hand. "Thank you so much, well, for everything," Paula said as she walked back to the car smiling. The waiter could not be sure, but he had a feeling that whoever this woman was that she had earlier bugged the table with a cell phone. He wondered if he should report this to the police, but then the man and the wealthy couple had been real jerks, ah, screw it, he thought to himself shaking his head.

48

While Dr Kirkland was out at the meeting, Daniel decided to use the time researching the make and model of the safe. After a quick internet search, he found the user guide online. He quickly read through the instructions for setting the combination. His eyes stopped when he reached the section describing the setting of the combination; The combination must be nine sets of numbers. This may include repeated number sets, read Daniel.

Getting out his notebook Daniel quickly drew a line through all the numbers that did not contain nine sets. What this didn't do was prove that any of the numbers he had tried so far was right, but it did weed out a whole lot of incorrect numbers, and that was something. Daniel looked at the clock on his computer. 2:45 pm, Yes, just enough time to have another look around Dr Kirkland's study. He thought to himself. This time Daniel concentrated on the desk and the contents of the draws. He carefully lifted items out one at a time and slowly read through each one hoping something would jump out. It was slow going and Daniel had to keep checking the time. Half an hour later he decided to give up before anyone came home. Back in his room he re-hid the notebook with the combinations and sat down at his desk in frustration.

Ash showered and got dressed, the black jeans and top had been replaced, this time she was wearing a dress. As Ash came into the kitchen, her father looked up from the newspaper he was reading. "Oh my God, are you sick?" he asked in shock.

"No, and stop it. It's a party for Daniel, I mean James, and you are driving us, remember?" Ash replied.

"I hadn't forgotten," Ben paused looking at his daughter, "Ash you look really nice. Standing there you remind me of your Mum. You look just like her," he remarked.

The smile on Ash's face faded, "I'm sorry dad, I didn't mean to upset you if you want I will go and change back into some jeans." Ash pleaded.

Ben spun around to face her, "Ash is that why you always wear black and dress like a boy? You're worried I will get upset when you remind me of your Mum?" he asked.

Ash sniffed back a tear, "I don't want to make you sad, and I know this sort of stuff reminds you of her," she replied.

Ben strode across the room and firmly held Ash by the shoulders. "Ashlie Grace Smith, you get this into your thick, stubborn, head. You walk in the room, and you remind me of Janice. You smile, and I see her like she is standing right here. The way you pout when you don't get your way. The way you tease me. How you look like crap when you get up. It's those things and a hundred others that every day remind me of your Mum. And I pray thanks to God that you keep doing that every day." Ben's voice had gone a bit hoarse.

Ash grabbed her Dad in a fierce hug, "I love you, Dad," she said breaking off and wiping tears from her face. "Now look what you have gone and done, this makeup stuff is running."

Ben put a hand up to his head, "Oh man, makeup, I'm getting the keys to the car, this is too much," he replied picking up the keys.

Ash had already organised the 'date' with Daniel, so it was no surprise when she and Ben pulled up outside his house. "See you later," he called leaving the house, as usual, there was no answer from Dr Kirkland. Daniel opened the back door and climbed in. Looking at Ash, his eyes went wide. "A Dress?" He asked.

Ash glared at him, "Shut up before I change my mind," she replied. "I didn't know you even owned a dress," Daniel stated, apparently still surprised.

"I went shopping, is that ok with you?" She asked clearly annoyed. Ben looked back in the rear-view mirror at Daniel grinning.

Ash stared back at her father, "You," She told him, "can just drive, not speak."

Ben grinned at her in the rear-view mirror, "As you wish," he replied using the line from her favourite film 'The Princes Bride'. As they drove off, Ash smiled at her father.

It didn't take long for Daniel to realise they were heading in the completely wrong direction for the movies. "So where are we going?" Daniel asked.

"We are going to pick up Gina and Steph," Ash replied.

Daniel cleared his throat, "Right, that sounds romantic, hanging out with my girlfriend and my… her friends." Daniel just caught himself just in time before he referred to Gina and Steph as his sisters.

"Just wait, I am sure there will be time for romance once we get to the movie," Ash replied. They pulled up at the motel and, both getting out, went to Gina and Steph's door and knocked.

Gina opened it, "Hey come on in," She said. Ash and Daniel went in Steph was putting some earrings on.

"Ready?" Ash asked.

Steph nodded, "Yup, come on through and say hi to Mom before we go. If you fail to do that she might just go back to Denver without you," Steph joked.

49

Daniel opened the internal door between the units. "Surprise!" they all shouted. The room was covered in decorations; there was a banner at the end of the room that read 'Happy 1st Birthday.' Underneath they had written each year, he had missed 2nd 3rd 4th, etc. through to 16th. The floor was entirely covered in inflated balloons to the extent you could not see it at all. Paula and Dennis stood over by a table full of presents and tears were streaming down Paula's face. Daniel waded through the balloons and with tears forming in his eyes, he gave Paula the biggest hug ever.

"I told myself I would not cry," Paula sobbed. "Happy birthday Daniel, this is for all the ones we have missed."

Dennis looked over at Ash, "Wow, you're wearing a dress," he stated.

Ash glared at Dennis, "If I hear one more person say I am wearing a dress, I am going to smack them in the face!" she announced laughing. Gina and Steph joined Paula and Daniel in one big group hug.

"I can't believe you have all done this for me," Daniel replied finally breaking up the hug.

"Presents," shouted Gina, "Come on, Presents!" They all waded over to the table full of gifts. Dennis pulled a chair out for Daniel while the girls sat on the floor amongst the balloons.

"This one first," Paula advised handing Daniel a small wrapped item. Daniel opened it by ripping the paper, something that would never be done at his old families events.

"Um, baby clothes?" he said holding up a small stretch and grow with a bemused look on his face.

"Now this one," Paula handed him a present that was in a box. Daniel ripped into this one as well.

"A pull along toy?" Daniel was starting to cotton on to what was happening. "These are all for each year I have missed, aren't they?" Paula nodded, "We didn't want you to miss out on any birthday, so we have got you a present that you would have been given at home with the girls," she explained.

Daniel didn't know who to hug first, "This is amazing, I love you all so much," he replied, hugging Paula again.

The gifts were incredible, Legos at five, Super Soakers at eight, football at nine. They just kept coming; Paula handed Daniel a small jewellery box, like a ring, would come in. It was not wrapped but had an elegant ribbon tied around it. Daniel undid the bow and opened the box. Sitting inside was a shiny gold key.

Daniel looked up at Paula and Dennis, "I don't think I understand?" he replied. Dennis came over to him, "It's the key to our house, Daniel. It's your key to your home."

Daniel shot to his feet, sending a wave of balloons over the girls, and grabbed Dennis in a huge hug. The two men stood there for what seemed like an age; no words were exchanged. The girls looked on, at a father, brother and boyfriend and there was not a dry face in the room.

As Dennis and Daniel broke out of the embrace Daniel spoke to Dennis with an emotional voice, "Do you think, when this is all sorted, I could have Farley as a surname?" Dennis grabbed Daniel back into another hug as Paula joined them. Tears flowed for minutes as the raw emotion of the day came flooding out.

Paula left the room to go and fetch the cake. "Dennis, I need your help." She called from the bedroom. Dennis came through to the bedroom with the sound of popping balloons and laughter following him. "Do I want to know?" asked Paula.

"Sitting on them is wildly fun, apparently," Dennis replied.

Paula smiled, "Loons, they are complete loons, but they are our loons," she replied, giving Dennis another hug.

"Here help me light these candles, there's too many for me to do it on my own." Dennis lit a match and started to light the candles. They were all in the shape of numbers from one to sixteen, and they covered the top of the cake.

"It looks crazy," Dennis commented. Once the candles were lit Dennis picked up the large cake and carried it out to the living area.

Paula started singing, "Happy Birthday to you…" The kids all stopped popping balloons to sing to Daniel. "Ok," Paula replied when the singing had finished, "Blow them out and make a wish." Daniel took a huge breath and blew all sixteen candles out in one blow to cheers and claps from his family and girlfriend.

Ash moved up to his side, "Did you make a wish?" she asked.

Daniel gestured to his family, "It already came true," he said hugging Ash. "Thank you for helping make this happen," he said.

"Hey I only lied to you so we could get you here," Ash grinned. "By the way, do you like me wearing a dress?" she asked.

"Like it? You look beautiful, but I think you look amazing in black as well." Daniel quickly dogged. Ash gave him a huge hug and leaning up gave him a big kiss. "I love you, Daniel Farley."

50

"How did the stakeout go today?" Daniel asked while eating a piece of cake.

Steph grinned, "We totally crushed it. We not only got great photos and video, but we recorded the sound as well."

"How did you get the audio?" Daniel asked.

"Mum and Dad duct taped a mobile phone under the table they were sitting at," Gina proudly announced.

Daniel grinned, "Who's inspired idea was that?" he asked.

Ash went red in the face as Gina pointed at her.

"Remind me never to cross you," Daniel said. "Do we have enough to convict him?" He asked.

"No, I don't think so, we have no other evidence other than the recording and Samantha's statement. I think a good lawyer would tear this to shreds in court," Dennis replied.

"Damn," Daniel replied, "I have tried every combination I could think of, and I can't get into the safe."

Dennis patted Daniel on the back, "Just remember Daniel, we don't even know if there is anything of use to us in there," Dennis pointed out. "You have to be careful not to put yourself at risk searching for somethings that may not even exist."

"Let's all meet over at Ash's tomorrow, and we can go over the photos again." Suggested Gina.

"Yea, ok," Daniel replied looking at his watch, "Hey we better get going, or Dr Kirkland will suspect something."

Paula grabbed her keys, and the twins stood up as if to go. "No you two stay here with Dennis and clean up, and don't forget the dishes!" Paula ordered.

"What, Daniel's had sixteen years of getting out of the dishes," Steph called out. "It's his birthday, and birthday boys don't do dishes!" Paula called over her shoulder grinning as she, Ash and Daniel walked out.

As the door closed, Dennis smiled at the girls.

"What's so funny Dad?" Steph asked.

"Well, I just thought that you are all triplets…"

Steph cut him off, "So?"

Dennis smiled again, "Well don't you all share the same birthday?" he replied.

Realisation dawned on Gina, "Mom's sneaky." Gina pointed out, collecting up broken balloons.

Dennis grinned, picking up some plates, "Yes, your Mum is sneaky, but you are still going to help clean up," Dennis replied laughing.

Paula dropped Ash and Daniel off at Ash's house. Daniel leant in the driver's window and gave Paula a kiss on the cheek. Paula began to tear up again.

"Don't worry; we will all be together permanently soon," Daniel pointed out. As they watched Paula drive off, Ash turned towards Daniel.

"What happens when this is over? I mean what happens to us?" She asked.

"I don't know Ash. So much has changed so quickly. I love you, and I don't want to leave, but I love my family two…" Daniel's voice trailed off.

Ash looked at Daniel, "I love you too, but I need you to know that I think your family should come first. It's not that far between Greenspan and Colorado. We could see one another some weekends. Do holidays and stuff."

Daniel took her hand and walked her to her door. "So this was meant to be a real date you know," Daniel said. "Hmm, yes, an actual date," Ash replied. Daniel stepped forward and took Ash in his arms he kissed her like he had never kissed before and Ash melted into his embrace.

She looked at Daniel as they parted, "Perhaps being a girl has some advantages, after all, night Daniel." Ash closed the door behind her and sighed.

51

"Have a nice night?" Ben asked from a comfortable chair across the room. "Dad! You gave me such a fright," Ash replied.

"Sorry, I was just sitting here reading," Ben replied.

"Sitting there waiting for your little girl to come home you mean," Ash stated.

"Yea, ok, busted, are you ok honey?" Ben asked. "Yes, I guess, well no not really," Ash crawled onto her father's lap.

"Cripes you have got big. So what's the prob?" he asked. Ash settled in; it felt right sitting like this, on her Dad's lap. "I love him Dad, and it hurts. He's leaving soon, and I don't want him to, but I have to keep telling him it's for the best. I'm lying to him Dad for his own good but all I want to do is tell him to stay," Ash replied.

"The Kirkland's are going away?" Ben asked.

"Yes, I think so," replied Ash, hoping the answer would not prompt more questions. "James is moving to Denver, Colorado."

Ben sat and thought for a moment, "Well Ash it's not that far, you could see one another if you took the bus. And what about that video thing, Skype? Couldn't you see him on that? You know Ash, if it's real, then distance shouldn't have anything to do with it."

Ash hugged her father tightly, "I love you, Dad."

"I love you two," Ben replied.

At 10 am the next day the doorbell rang. "Hi James, come on in," Ben said seeing who it was. "How was last night?" he asked.

"Like nothing I have ever seen, just crazy Mr Smith. Ash around?" Daniel asked.

"Think she is just finishing up in the shower. So what's on the cards for today?" Ben asked.

"Oh, Ash invited me, Gina and Steph over to work on that mystery safe thing," Daniel replied.

"Right, so you haven't figured it out yet then?" Ben asked.

Daniel crashed down onto the sofa, "Nope, tried lots of numbers like birthdays and stuff like that. I think it has to be in plain sight, but we just haven't found the clue yet," Daniel replied as the doorbell rang again.

Ben let Gina and Steph in, "Hi guys," he said as they came in.

"Hi Mr Smith," they said in unison.

"You do that often, answer at the same time?" Ben asked smiling. "More often than you would believe," Gina replied laughing.

"Right then I will leave you to it. Let me know if you want snacks or drinks," Ben offered as he went back out to the kitchen.

Ash came down the stairs to find all three of the Farley's sitting around the TV. "Hey, give me a moment, and I will get the laptop," Ash said heading back up the stairs. She was back down in a few minutes with the laptop and a cable to connect it to the TV.

"So I have found out that the safe uses a nine number combination, each number can be between one and thirty," Daniel explained. "Well that must have knocked off a few numbers," Gina stated.

"It did, but none of the other numbers worked either," Daniel replied. They continued to pour over the images looking for anything they had missed. About an hour in Ben returned to the room. Gina, Steph and Daniel were all writing down combinations on pieces of paper.

"Look at you lot," Ben said.

"What?" Steph asked, apparently confused. Ben pointed to the three Farley kids, "All writing with your left hands, suspicious," Ben replied.

"Huh? What's suspicious?" Ash asked hopeful her dad had not figured it out.

Ben laughed, "Suspicious is what they used to call people with left-handedness. There is usually only one person in every eight who has it. So these three are obviously all suspicious," He replied. The triplets all looked at each other with a look of concern, followed by relief as they understood Ash's dad had not found them out. Ben noticed the look, but could not put his finger on what was going on. Looking down at the numbers on their pages, he commented on their progress, "So any luck yet? He asked.

"No we still haven't found a thing," Ash replied. "Show me the picture," Ben asked. "There's more than one," Ash countered.

"Ok let have a quick look," Ben clicked between each of the images, "Most people hide stuff in plain sight," he said, "especially if the combination is tricky to remember. Hey, what about the Humidor?" Ben asked pointing to the wooden box on Dr Kirkland's desk. "What's a humidor?" Daniel asked.

"It's where people store cigars, to keep them in the right condition with the right amount of moisture, it stops them drying out," Ben replied.

"But Dad doesn't smoke cigars," Daniel replied, not realising his slip-up. Ben looked at Daniel but didn't say anything; something was going on here. Ben decided he was going to have a little chat to Ash shortly, but he wanted to do that alone, right now he was going to listen and see what else these kids let slip.

"But those are just letters," Daniel stated.

"Yes they are, but if you substitute numbers for letters like 1 for A, 2 for B, 3 for C, well you get the picture. You've got a code." Ben replied. "We use to do stuff like this in Eagle Scouts," Ben explained.

"Pass me some pen and paper!" Gina demanded.

The label on the humidor was 'Cigar Saint Luis Rey - Lonsdale's'. "The full name is way too long, what about the type of cigar?" Daniel asked. Gina created a matrix of letters on the page and then assigned them numbers. She then wrote out 'L o n s d a l e s' with a space between each letter. Matching the letters to the numbers was now easy, and after a few moments they had the following numbers written above; 12, 15, 14, 19, 4, 1, 12, 5, 19.

Steph counted the number groups up, "Nine" she announced. Ben watched as the teens looked at one another. Whatever was going on here, Ben knew they thought that they had just scored a major victory.

"Right well, I better get going and write this answer up for tomorrow," Daniel announced.

"Hey us two. Mum wanted us home as soon as we had figured it out," Steph said.

"Hey, thanks, Mr Smith," Gina said as her, and Steph headed to the door with Daniel. As she spoke Ben looked at the three of them, Wow they look like they are related, he thought. Like peas and a pod. Ash got up and saw them out, pausing to give Daniel a quick kiss as he left.

52

Ash turned back into the room, and her father was standing in the middle of the room, his hand on his hips, not a good sign, Ash knew. "Ok, what the hell is going on Ash? And don't give me the bs line that this is just homework," Ben ordered.

Ash sighed. "I think you need to sit down," she replied.

Ben sat back on the sofa, "Are you in trouble Ash?" he asked looking very concerned.

Ash stayed standing, "No but Daniel is," she replied.

"You mean James is in trouble?" he asked.

Ash took a seat on the other sofa, "No Dad, Daniel is in trouble. His real name is Daniel Johnson. He is Gina and Steph's brother. They're triplets," Ash let the bombshell hang for a few moments. "The twins and James, are related?" he asked, clearly having trouble taking it all in.

Ash nodded, "Yes James, who is really Daniel, is Paula and Dennis Farley's son. He was stolen at birth from a clinic in Denver, Colorado by Dr and Mrs Kirkland. We have been trying to get some evidence to build a case against Dr Kirkland," she explained.

"Are you crazy Ash? Have you heard what you are saying?" Ben stood up and picked up his keys.

"Where are you going?" Ash asked, concern showing on her face. "Not just me sunshine, we are both going to see the Farley's right now." Ben near dragged Ash to the car, and they sat in silence as they drove over to the Motel.

Ben parked the car right outside Paula's room and headed to the door. "Hello, can I help you, Oh hi Ash," Dennis said when he opened the door.

"Mr Farley this is my Dad, Ben. He knows, I had to tell him," Ash walked in past Dennis and sat down on a chair at the table.

Ben stood at the door not moving. It was as if coming in would prove what Ash had said. "What the hell is going on Mr Farley?" Ben asked.

"You better come in Mr?" Dennis asked, not knowing Ash's surname.

"Smith." Ben finished for him. As Ben stepped through the door, Paula came out of the bedroom. "Who was at the door…" her voice trailed off. "Ash, Officer Smith." Paula finished while looking at Ash for some clue as to why they were there.

"Dad figured some of it out, so I told him the rest, and now he doesn't believe me," Ash had slumped into the chair looking very dejected.

"How about I make us all some coffee, Dennis call the girls in, they need to be here two," Paula instructed.

Ben came over to the table and sat down next to Ash. Dennis knocked on the interior door and called the girls. A moment passed then Gina and Steph came in. Ben could still not get over how identical they looked. It was not just the physical appearance either. It was the way they moved, their mannerisms, it was like they were two parts of one unit, completely in sync. Watching them come in, Ben thought back to when he saw the three kids together at home. My God, he thought, they are related. Seeing them all together you could see the resemblance, but it wasn't just that, all three had moved the same way, they had the same mannerisms. Ben looked over to Paula who was bringing a jug and some cups to the table. "It's true isn't it?" Ben asked. Paula nodded and sat down. "How did it happen?" he asked.

"I was seventeen, and I had a fling with an older guy. It was a one-time thing, and he didn't want commitment. I found out about ten weeks later that I was pregnant and let's just say he didn't want kids either. My family and friends threatened to cut me off if I didn't have an abortion. There was no way I could ever have an abortion, so they cut me off. They have never met the girls. I found this clinic that specialised in multiple birth pregnancy. When it came time to deliver the triplets they told me, there were complications with one of the babies. I was rushed in for a c-section and had a general anaesthetic. When I recovered, I was told only Gina and Steph had survived," Paula paused. This was still raw for her; Ben could see.

Dennis came over and sat next to Paula putting his hand on hers in a gesture of support. Paula continued, "It was by pure chance that about eight weeks ago I recognised the nurse from the clinic at a coffee shop, and she slipped me a note," Paula stood up and got her bag, retrieved the note and gave it to Ben.

Taking the note, Ben relieved his glasses from his pocket, "You met this woman? He asked after reading the note.

Paula nodded. "She has become a Christian and needed to put this right." Ben nodded as Paula explained Samantha's motivation for coming clean and trying to make amends.

"Samantha has provided us with a signed affidavit," Dennis advised, handing over the typed and signed document.

Ben looked up from the signed document, "I don't understand, why not go straight to the police. Surely a DNA test would put this to bed," he asked.

53

The Farley's and Ash looked at one another; it was Ash that broke the silence. "Dad, Daniel was not the only baby that was stolen," Ash let this bit of news sink in.

Ben looked shocked, "There were more, how many more? What proof do you have?" he asked.

"Samantha told us there were more. He has been selling babies for years," Paula replied.

"And the other day we recorded this," Gina said, placing the dictaphone on the table and pressing play.

Ben listened to the full recording while sipping his coffee. "This is dynamite if you had video it would be enough to convict," Ben pointed out.

Ash grinned at her father, "Oh we have video," she said proudly. Ben looked at Ash and the twins, "You got all this by yourselves?" He asked shaking his head.

"Well we had some help from Mr and Mrs Farley, they planted the mobile phone," Ash explained.

Ben sat thinking for a moment. "The safe," he suddenly blurted out, "James has been trying to crack Dr Kirkland's safe," Ben asked, though it was more of a statement than a question.

Ash nodded, "We think there might be evidence of the other abductions. If we can find it, we can not only stop it happening again but fix what Kirkland has done."

Dennis had sat there mostly quiet through this discussion.

"Ben, how legal is this evidence?" he asked.

Ben thought for a moment. "Technically the affidavit is legal but very easy to disprove; they just have to imply malice; you know unhappy employee wants revenge, that sort of thing happens all the time. The recording is good and should hold," Ben replied.

"But what about if Daniel finds something in the safe? Can it be used in court, if it has been stolen?" Dennis asked.

Ben shook his head, "Taking the items from the safe would be considered theft, but the judge would not care how the object was discovered once it is brought into evidence. If James, I mean Daniel can get it then we can use it," Ben announced.

"You're going to help?" Ash asked her dad. "I don't see how I can't help Ash, if what you claim is true and it does sound true, then Dr Kirkland needs to face justice," Ben replied.

"But Daniel's right in the middle of this, you can't go arresting Dr Kirkland right now," Paula pleaded.

Ben laughed, "Mrs Farley, it might seem like we just charge in like CSI Miami with guns blazing, but it's just not how it happens in real life. To be honest, this is going to take me at least a few days just to prepare the paperwork to present to my captain. Add to that a couple of days for a search warrant and then an arrest warrant. No, we are looking at the better part of a week or more before we go knocking on Dr Kirkland's door," Ben smiled at Paula, who was looking quite worried. "But if I think James, drat this is going to take some getting use to, Daniel is at risk; I will go in all guns blazing. That's my promise to you."

Paula got up and came around to Ben and gave him a big hug. "Thank you, Officer Smith," she said.

"Call me Ben." he replied.

"That sounds better, thank you, Ben, and please call us Paula and Dennis," Dennis replied.

54

Simon glanced at his calendar, as was his habit first thing Monday. There were the usual staff meetings, clinical rounds and tonight a meeting with Pullman. Simon then logged into the practice computer and scanned the appointments for the coming week. One meeting on Wednesday looked promising, a single pregnant woman carrying twins, due in three months, That's soon. Simon thought to himself opening the records to have a closer look. Ah, there's the reason, just moved into the area. This could be perfect. He thought. Simon printed out the file and stored it in his briefcase and headed off to the clinic for the day.

Daniel sat at the kitchen table eating his breakfast as Dr Kirkland came in dressed in a robe. "Hello James, how did you sleep?" he asked. Before James could answer, "I have a dinner meeting tonight." he explained. Daniel noted the usual lack of concern on how or what he would eat for dinner.

"Ok, hope your meeting goes well," he replied as Dr Kirkland left the room. Perfect, Daniel thought to himself; it would allow time to try the safe combination and have a proper search.

After breakfast, Daniel walked over to Ash's house and knocked on the door. Ash came to the door with a big smile on her face. "Hey, what's going on?" Daniel asked noticing Ash was wearing a dress again.

"Well, it has been an exciting weekend. You like?" Ash asked twirling her dress.

"Um, yes, what's the occasion?" Daniel replied.

"Well yesterday you let slip that your ‘dad' doesn't smoke cigars, and well my Dad cottoned on so I told him the truth," Ash grinned as she dropped the bombshell.

Daniel was gobsmacked. "You told your Dad?"

"Yup, and then he dragged me over to your parents motel, and they confirmed the whole story," Ash replied grinning.

"Ash, How is this funny, your Dad is going to blow the whole thing," Daniel raged.

"Settle down Daniel, Dad has started an investigation; no one else is involved, yet. He needs you to get more evidence," she explained. Daniel relaxed, "Dr Kirkland's out tonight. You want to help me search for that evidence?" he asked.

"You're on, what time?" she asked. "About 6:30 pm, the good Doctor has a dinner meeting," Daniel explained as they walked, hand in hand, to school.

55

The day had been productive for Simon. The potential new target looked promising, and that should keep the Fletchers happy. Simon arrived home and headed to his study. Locking the door, he opened the safe and removed a notebook. Simon turned on the photocopier and waited while it copied the pages from 1997. He figured he would need to provide these to Pullman. The copies he placed into his briefcase and then returned the notebook back to the safe. Simon looked at his watch, 5:49 pm. Better get going, he thought to himself, that flea bitten dinner was on the outskirts of town. Simon picked up his briefcase and headed for his car.

Driving out to the diner Simon noted his mileage. 22,000 miles, about time I traded this for something a bit newer. Perhaps something sporty like a Porsche 911 Turbo. After all, he could well afford it, what with all the money hidden away in his 'special' account in the Caymans. That was part of his exit plan if it all went south. There was a false passport for him, and James in the safe and $150,000 in cash. Simon could have them in the Cayman's in under a day; the flight was just under three hours, and there was a twice daily service out of Houston. Once in the Cayman's they would live very comfortably on his ill-gotten gains. Simon arrived at the Old Coach Road diner.

It was typical of this kind of establishment. Catering to truck drivers, and a few locals. It was an excellent location for a meeting if you didn't want to be remembered. The food and service were also typical. Simon wondered if he would get food poisoning eating here. Parking just off the road Simon walked the last hundred feet or so to the dinner, not wanting his car to stand out. Looking at the other vehicles parked out front he realised what a good decision that was. Almost everyone was a pickup truck, and his BMW certainly would have caused people to talk.

Simon opened the door and began to scan the room for Pullman. He spotted him sitting in a slightly darker corner away from other patrons. Simon walked over to the corner. "Dr Kirkland. How are you sir," Derrick Pullman stood up and thrust out a giant hand to shake Simon's.

"Fine, fine, thank you," Simon replied inwardly wincing with the force of Pullman's grip.

Pullman released Simon's hand and sat back down indicating for him to do the same. "So what will you have to drink?" Pullman asked.

"Um, I think I am fine at present," Simon replied.

Pullman shook his head, "Nonsense, can't come to a place like this and not have a drink, people might talk," Pullman said the last part quieter with almost a threat in his voice.

"Ok, a Merlot then," Simon replied.

"Ha, that's a good one, red wine in a place like this," Pullman laughed smacking his hand on the table. Pullman waved a busty waitress over.

"What can I do for you gentlemen?" she asked. "Well, let's just start with drinks sugar, two whiskies, straight up," Pullman replied eyeing up the woman's ample cleavage. Simon inwardly recoiled, the man disgusted him, not only were his manners atrocious but his looks also. Each time

Pullman opened his mouth, he revealed horribly stained yellow teeth, and the stench of bad breath carried towards Simon. Just when he thought he had got used to the smell it wafted in again threatening to make him gag.

"So what can I do for you, Dr Kirkland?" Pullman asked after the waitress had brought them their drinks.

Simon handed Pullman the photocopied pages from the notebook and the names of the Farley family. "I need you to find out anything you can about this family." He said pointing to the Farley's names.

"What's the photocopied stuff?" Pullman asked eyeing the copies of the notebook pages.

"That's the problem, I think they might be the same people, and it's important that I find out," Derrick nodded, he was one of the few people who knew the extent of Simon's crimes. Simon had used him on almost every transaction to ensure all parties remained quiet. At the very least, Derrick Pullman was hired to check out potential new clients to ensure Simon was not setup.

"These people have anything to do with your son?" Pullman asked.

Pullman may have been a grotesques example of a man, but his looks hid a sharp mind.

Simon nodded, "Perhaps, and that's why this needs to be handled quickly and cleanly. I don't want any loose ends," Simon stated as he pushed over an envelope to Pullman. Derrick pocketed the envelope without opening it; he knew it would contain at least fifteen thousand dollars. With this amount of cash on the line and a similar payment that he knew he would get if he were successful, Derrick was going to put his other cases, mostly Bond skips, on ice while he chased down the information Dr Kirkland required.

"Always a pleasure Dr Kirkland," Pullman announced peeling a twenty out of his wallet for the drinks. "I will get back to you as soon as possible."

56

Ash waited until she saw Dr Kirkland drive past then headed over to Daniel's. She tapped on the door, and he opened it up. "Ready?" She asked giving him a kiss.

"Never been more so," Daniel announced. They headed straight to Dr Kirkland's study, and Daniel turned on the lights. Daniel lifted the family painting off the wall again, noting how it was hanging tonight. Ash could see the safe mounted into the wall. Daniel handed her a slip of paper with the combination. "You read them, and I will try the dial," he said.

Ash paused between each number, "12, 15, 14, 19, 4, 1, 12, 5, 19, that's it," she said at the end.

Daniel looked over at Ash, "This still might not be the right number," he stated.

"Oh for Pete sake, just open the damn thing, Daniel!" Ash said becoming quite frustrated. Daniel grasped the handle and twisted it down. With an audible click the door of the safe swung open. Ash gave Daniel a big hug. "We've done it!"

"Yes, but what have we found?" Daniel asked.

They carefully took each item out one at a time. The first item was a notebook. Ash thumbed through the pages, "It's names and dates, and family names of the people who purchased the babies," Ash announced. "We got it, 1997!" She said excitedly, "Daniel, this is the entry about you, Gina, Steph and Paula, it's all here."

Daniel stood in shock. "I can't believe we found it first up. Quick we need a copy. Copy every page," he said to Ash. Daniel continued to look through the safe. There were two notebooks spanning twenty years. Two floppy disks a CD-ROM, and a USB memory stick. "We are going to need to copy all of this stuff as well," Daniel said holding it up for Ash to see.

She nodded, "You go and get your laptop, and we can at least copy the CD and memory stick," Ash suggested. Daniel ran upstairs and grabbed his laptop. Ash had finished copying the notebooks, and she was examining the last items in the safe when Daniel returned. "Hey Jamie," Ash said showing Daniel a fake passport with his photo in. "That's my photo. What the hell?" Daniel exclaimed. "Shall we take these and the money?" Ash asked.

Daniel came over to look at the envelope, "The money, what money?" he asked.

"This money." Ash showed Daniel an envelope chock full of $100 bills. "I think this is his plan if he gets caught. Fake passports and a heap of cash would help him get pretty much anywhere. We take them, and we stop him from running," Ash explained.

"Won't he notice they're missing?" Daniel asked as he was copying the files onto his computer.

Ash shook her head, "Doubt it; the passports were in the envelope with the cash. We will just stuff something about the same size in and pile the rest back on top," Ash grinned. Walking over to the bookshelf she scanned the titles looking for a book about the right size. Ash laughed as she took a book down from the shelf. After rearranging the remaining books, no one would know there was one missing. "How about this then?" Ash asked showing Daniel the title; 'The HMS Revenge'.

Daniel just about choked on his laugh. "Oh, that is just perfect." Daniel slid the book into the envelope and placed it back into the safe. He then loaded the USB memory stick and CD Rom. Daniel indicated to Ash, "The USB thing is encrypted," he advised. "Just copy it anyway, perhaps it can be hacked, we will give it to my dad," Ash replied.

Ash gathered up all the notebooks and making sure they were in the correct order put them back in as well. Daniel then closed the safe and returned the family portrait. "Right let's get out of here before we get caught," Ash said.

Back in his room Daniel copied the files to a spare USB memory stick and gave them to Ash, "Get these to your Dad," Daniel instructed.

"What you're not coming. We've got what we need, you can get out of here and go join your family," Ash said.

"Not yet, I need to give your Dad as much time as possible to build the case. If I disappear now, he will know something is up, and he will bolt," Daniel replied.

Ash knew he was right. "Daniel Farley, the moment Dad has a case we are pulling you out, and not a moment longer," Ash kissed him. "Stay safe," She said as she climbed out the window.

Ash rushed back to her house and her Dad. Ben was sitting watching TV when she ran into the living room.

"We got it all!" Ash exclaimed. "What did you get?" Ben asked excitedly.

"Notebooks with names and dates, a CD with the same sort of stuff and a USB Stick," Ash explained. "Oh, and these," Ash said handing her father the fake passports and the money.

"You kids have done so well. This is exactly what I need to build an iron-tight case," Ben replied.

Ash looked a bit concerned, "Dad, Daniel stayed behind. He won't pull out until you have a case," Ben looked at his daughter, "I promise you I will make this happen as quickly as possible. Remember he should be okay as long as Dr Kirkland doesn't know that we are aware," Ben didn't believe in spinning it for his daughter, she knew the risks as well as him.

57

Derrick Pullman was good at what he did. If you wanted someone found, he was your man. After leaving the Old Coach Road dinner, he headed back to the office. 'No time like the present' he was often heard to quote, and to Derrick, time was money. Clients often paid bonuses for him quickly delivering what they wanted, and none paid better than Dr Simon Kirkland. Stuck up toff Pullman thought to himself. But he was a toff with money, and that was the only requirement to Derrick Pullman.

Sitting down at his computer he started a search for Paula Johnson. As he expected, this returned an enormous number of hits. Opening another tab, he entered Paula Farley and hit search. This also brought back a raft of hits. Drumming his fingers on the desk, Derrick opened two more tabs and repeated the same two searches, this time adding 'Denver' to them both. The number of hits reduced dramatically. Derrick then switched each of last two search results to image search.

His screen filled up with pictures of women named Paula Farley and Paula Johnson. Derrick clicked between the last two tabs, jumping back and forward between each. Bingo, he thought to himself. Derrick clicked on one of the Paula Farley images and was taken to an article in the Denver Post. The article was a local business story about a single mother of twins who had married her college professor and now ran a very successful antique business.

Derrick picked up the phone and dialled a number from memory, "Hello Grant Tolstrom, Texas DMV." Derrick heard down the line, "Grant it's Derrick, I need you to run some licences." Derrick replied "No prob, regular deal?"

"Yip, $300 per name, write these down. Paula Farley and Paula Johnson. Both of Denver Colorado. You got my fax number?" Derrick asked.

"Yes, unless you've changed it. Give me ten minutes; I'll see what I can dig up," Tolstrom replied.

Derrick hung up. He had a deal with Tolstrom, a slightly corrupt official, at the department of motor vehicles. For a small sum, a charge that Pullman would be passing on to his client as an expense, he would get a full copy of the targets drivers licence, the details of any vehicles they owned and their home address. To Pullman, it was good value and often a great place to start when trying to locate someone.

Derrick didn't think it would come to anything, but he tried the same internet search with the first name of Philippa. As he expected, there were no duplicate pictures on either image search. The fax in the corner of the office began to ring, and once connected started printing out. At the same time, the phone rang. "Derrick Pullman Investigations," Derrick answered.

"Hey Derrick, it's Grant, what are you pulling?" Tolstrom asked.

"What do you mean?" Derrick asked.

"Those two people you wanted info on, well they are the same person," Derrick grinned to himself as Grant continued. "Paula Johnson is Paula Farley. Farley is her married name. I'm faxing you the details now, including her registration for her car. Is that what you wanted? I have a feeling you know this stuff already," Tolstrom remarked.

Derrick chuckled, "No, I didn't know, but I had a pretty good hunch. Thanks for getting back to me so fast. I will send you your fee in cash, thanks again." Derrick hung up and crossed over to the fax machine and removed three pages. The top page was a copy of the registration papers for a red 2001 VW Golf in the name of Paula Farley.

The next page was a copy of Paula's licence in her maiden name of Johnson, and the final page was her current licence, surname Farley. Got you, Derrick said to himself. The pieces start to fit together. Paula Johnson just happens to turn up in the same town as Dr Kirkland. Derrick thought to himself; she has got to know about the baby. But how could she know? Only a very few people were involved. Derrick sat back down and reviewed the copy of the notebook page. Kirkland had recorded all the staff who were involved and what they had been paid. One name stood out, Samantha Scott.

58

It was one of the first jobs Kirkland had asked Derrick to perform. He was worried that one of his ex-staff would talk, so he asked Derrick to go and have a little chat with the nurse in question. Derrick had taken particular enjoyment tormenting Nurse Scott. He left little notes saying things like; "I know what you have done, tell no one". Or "you are being watched." It all came to a head when Derrick followed her home from work one night and had a face to face chat with Miss Scott.

Derrick had loved the look of fear in her eyes as he held his knife to her throat. He calmly explained what would happen if she ever spoke of what she had done or seen. Derrick had punched her savagely in the stomach and left her doubled up on the ground, while he walked off back to his car. It would seem that Miss Scott had not learnt her lesson. Derrick smiled to himself. Well, we will see about that, and we will find out what she has said and to whom. Derrick was looking forward to this little reunion.

It took another three hundred dollars passed to Grant Tolstrum at the DMV, and half an hour to locate Samantha Scott. Derrick was unable to find out where she worked, but he was sure that he would be able to follow her from her home without being seen. Opening up his computer Derrick logged into the Amtrak website to search for trains. Damn it! Amtrak didn't have a route between Dallas and Denver. Derrick switched to American Airways. I hate flying, he thought to himself. Oh well, at least it was faster than driving or the train. Derrick selected a flight and booked a rental car. Three days ought to do it, he decided.

Sitting in the aeroplane, Derrick considered if he should update Simon Kirkland. No, better to have the whole story and get paid for all the work, he mused. Derrick gripped the seat arms as some turbulence jolted the aeroplane. Derrick could face any danger but when it came to flying he would go weak with fear. Flying was not natural, something hanging up there with nothing visible holding it up. Derrick thought, another jolt making him grip harder. At least it was a short flight, only just over two hours, and not over water.

On arrival, Derrick walked straight off the plane as he only had his carry-on with him. Picking up a map and the rental car took him over forty-five minutes, but the car was a tidy and nondescript Ford sedan. As Derrick had flown, he needed to find a gun store. Derrick located one within ten minutes and with a fake ID he had a Taurus 738 TCP .380 cal pistol tucked into his belt, he would bill this to Dr Kirkland as well. The Taurus was tiny in comparison to what he had in his safe, but it was small, cheap and very common. It would have to be ditched before he returned to Texas, but that was just how it went, besides Kirkland would be billed for any extra expenses. Derrick didn't think he would need it, but he felt naked without a piece.

It was four in the afternoon when Derrick pulled up a few doors away from Samantha's flat. With no idea where she worked or what she did Derrick could be waiting a while. He removed his seat belt and made himself more comfortable. This was always the worst part of a stakeout, Derrick's large frame made waiting for long periods very uncomfortable. Derrick could kill for a coffee right now, but that would only make the need to pee later on. It was a part of stakeout that Hollywood never showed. Sitting for hours in a car then having got pee in a bottle. Yea that would make great a great NCIS episode. Derrick chuckled to himself. No, it was just better to grit and bear it. A drink would come after he had tracked her down. Derrick glanced at the clock on the dash, 4:58 pm; it would be dark soon, and less likely Samantha would be easy to spot. The another side of the coin was it would mean Samantha would probably not see Derrick. This job was full of double-edged swords. Derrick thought to himself.

59

Samantha's arms hurt, a full shift at the cafe then a short trip to the supermarket for essentials. Essentials, why does a trip to the store for milk and bread end up with two full bags of food? She thought as she lugged them home. At least I will have worked off that tub of ice-cream nestled in one of the bags. Samantha grinned thinking of the little treat she was going to reward herself with when she got home. Arriving at her flat Sam put her bags down and opened her door.

Parked further down the road, Derrick watched Samantha through a pair of Zeiss Terra compact binoculars. Their large diameter front elements allowed plenty of light to enter and saved Derrick from needing low light or night vision gear. "Yes, I remember you, Miss Scott. But it seems you have forgotten the rules," Derrick muttered to himself. "But I will help jog your memory; you will remember the rules when I have finished with you." Derrick started the car; he would be back tomorrow to follow her to her work; he would then have a look around her flat to see if he could work out who or if she had talked to anyone.

Samantha locked the door behind her and carried the shopping bags to the kitchen counter. Her flat may have been small, but she kept it clean and tidy. Sam put the groceries away in the kitchen and placed the 'treat' ice-cream into the freezer. Not feeling like dinner yet, Sam took out her new Apple laptop and checked her email. Twenty-eight messages popped up, and as she scanned through them, she deleted the spam messages that seemed to clutter her inbox more and more each day. One message stood out from the others; it was from Paula Farley. Sam double clicked the email to open it. It was an update from the Farley's.

Things were going well, Daniel, James Farley's real name, now knew the truth and was helping to gather evidence against the Kirkland's along with his girlfriend, Ashlie. They had even thrown Daniel a one to sixteenth birthday party for all the ones he had missed. Paula went on to say that they were pretty sure that this would all be over soon and they would come back to Denver. Paula signed off saying how thankful they all were for Sam's courage coming forward and that she was completely forgiven. Tears streamed down Sam's face. Heading back to the freezer, Sam decided to skip dinner and go straight to the ice-cream. Grabbing a spoon and the ice-cream, Sam sat back down to reread the email from Paula.

Derrick returned the next day at 8:30 am and waited in the rental car. At 8:42 am he saw Samantha leave her flat and walk off in the opposite direction. Derrick waited half a minute before exiting the car and following her at a distance. He was far enough behind Samantha not be noticed. He was just another person out for a walk in the morning. Four blocks on and the surroundings merged from built-up residential to office spaces and shops. Samantha turned and entered a coffee shop.

Derrick held back and found a seat at a bus stop on the other side of the road. Ten minutes past and Derrick was getting worried that he had been made, perhaps she had seen him and exited the coffee shop out another door. Derrick crossed the road and walked towards the coffee shop. As he passed, he noticed that there were very few customers inside. He glanced at the tables as he checked out the breakfast menu in the window. Samantha hadn't sat down anywhere in the cafe. Damn! Derrick thought as he turned to leave. Just then he turned and saw one of the waitresses. Surprise registered on his face as he recognised Samantha standing behind the counter. Derrick walked on, So that is why she didn't come up during his search for nurses. He thought to himself. Perhaps she has had a crisis of confidence and had given up nursing? Derrick chuckled to himself. No matter, He would find out all tonight when he paid her a little personal visit.

Derrick drove the rental back to Samantha's house and parked down the street. Casually walking up to her flat he fished out his lock picks. The door posed no real challenge and Derrick was inside in under half a minute. Derrick closed the door behind him and re-locked it. He glanced around the room, searching for an alarm panel. "That makes it easy," he said to himself not finding one.

Derrick wandered around the flat, not touching anything at first, just looking, getting a feel for the place. Samantha kept her place pretty clean and tidy. There were no dishes in the kitchen sink. Derrick opened the refrigerator, no signs of taking out, just yoghurt, vegetables, fruit and other healthy foods. Opening the icebox, he noticed a tub of ice-cream and some frozen cuts of meat. No, it looked like Miss Scott lived simply but well. Her flat was the complete opposite of his. No plates with leftover take out on the coffee table. No stubbed out cigarette butts dropped into part drunk coffee cups.

Derrick moved off to the bedroom, again here the room was well kept. The bed was made, the drapes pulled back. On the dressing table were the usual assortments of beauty products, moisturisers, makeup removal wipes, perfumes and a stand of necklaces and hoop earrings. Beside her bed, Derrick discovered a Mac laptop. It was one of those ultra-thin models that looked like it was impossible to fit all the bits inside. Derrick sat down on the bed and opened up the laptop; it powered up almost instantly. Great, no password, he smiled, thinking to himself, that makes my job easier. Even though Derrick was not used to the Mac, it did not take him long to find what he was looking for, the email program. Clicking on the little postage stamp icon, the email program popped up on screen. As it opened the laptop connected to the mail server and downloaded ten messages. Derrick could see that they were mostly spam. Scanning the titles of the previous emails Derrick stopped and double clicked on one, in particular, the sender was Paula Farley.

To: sam.i.am57@aol.com

From: paula.farley.family@gmail.com

Subject: Progress

Hi Sam

Just thought you would like a quick update on where we are at. The girls and I have shifted down to Texas to try and get to know Daniel. It has been so much more of a success than we had ever hoped. If Daniel, who the Kirkland's call James, had been happy and settled then I think I could have left it there, but sadly this was not the case. He needs us as much as we need him. Well, long story short, Daniel now knows the truth, and with his girlfriend Ash, they have secured evidence that will put Dr Kirkland away for good.

Last week we held a one to sixteen birthday for Daniel. This was to make up for all the years we have missed. We all had such a great time. The twins were able to get video of another of Dr Kirkland's business dealings so with the evidence, Daniel and Ash have, what we have collected and your affidavit, we should have a rock solid case. We are going to ensure you are safe from prosecution when we hand over the stuff to the police.

You may have helped make this happen, but you have done the right thing by telling us the truth, and I want you to know I, well we, forgive you. You have brought our family back together, Sam and we thank you. By the way, the twins, or should I call them the triplets, have the strangest connection. If one of them gets hurt, the others feel it too. It is weird to see it in action; Steph jabbed a thumb tack into her leg, and Gina and Daniel almost shot through the roof. It would seem they were meant to be together.

Well, it looks like I am babbling, I must admit that I am still on cloud nine having held my not so little boy finally so that I will finish this email here. We hope to be back soon, and we would love it if you would come and visit us.

Blessings

Paula, Dennis, Gina, Steph and Daniel

60

Derrick felt his skin crawl. The Farley's not only knew, but they also had evidence. Could this evidence be traced back to him? No doubt that prick Kirkland would have records of the payments he had made. It would not take a particularly bright investigator to connect the dots and end up with a visit from the police. Crap, he thought to himself he was going to have a little chat with Samantha here, but this didn't look like it could wait. Derrick quickly emailed himself a copy of the message from Paula Farley, then spent the next ten precious minutes trying to work out how to delete any sign he had sent it.

After finally working out the procedure he replaced the laptop beside the bed after wiping it down to remove any prints. Derrick let himself out the door and casually walked back to his rental car. He may have looked casual to an observer, but his heart was running at a million miles an hour as he searched for a way to get out of harm's way. "Curse bloody Kirkland," He said under his breath. "When this is over I'm paying him a visit, this is going to cost him, one way or another!"

Derrick drove back into town and parked one street on the main street of shops and businesses. He was going to have to wait a while, Best I figure out when Samantha is finishing work. He thought to get out of the car. Derrick walked back to the main street and searched for a telephone box. He quickly scanned the phone book for the cafe's number. Fishing for a quarter in his pocket he deposited it into the pay phone.

"Hi, Main Street Cafe, how can I help you," Came a cheerful voice. "Oh, hello, I wondered if you could tell me your opening hours?" Derrick asked.

"Sure no problem, we are open 8 am to 5 pm Monday to Friday, and 8 am to 1:30 pm Saturdays, would you like to make a book…." Derrick cut her off replacing the receiver. He looked at his watch, 10:45 am, Crap, ages to wait, he thought. What am I supposed to do until 5 pm? Derrick looked around, slightly down the street he noticed a strip bar. That'll do. He wondered down to see if they were open.

The atmosphere was like many of these places; cigarette smoke clouded the air, and his shoes stuck to the floor that had seen too many spilt drinks and too few thorough cleanings. There was a single stripper doing a pole dance routine in the centre of an island stage, and to Derrick, she looked only slightly cleaner than the floor. Over the years Derrick had taken a shine to high-class hookers or escorts as he called them. The funds he secured from Dr Kirkland and others allowed him to indulge in this pricey hobby not nearly as often as he liked. But like a hardened drug addict, he now looked at the cheaper product with a cynical eye.

The bare-chested woman, gyrating on the pole, did nothing for him. Derrick ordered a double whisky straight up. As he drank his second, third and fourth drinks, he became madder and madder at the thought that this chubby whore was all that he might be able to afford in the future. Kirkland, the Farley's, that Ash girl and Samantha Scott, were all to blame, and they would all pay. By the time 4:30 pm rolled around Derrick was well liquored up good and proper. Derrick paid the bill and wandered outside to wait for Samantha in an ally that Sam would have to pass on her way home. Derrick leant up against the red brick wall of a nearby shop and waited.

At about 5 pm the traffic had built up into a steady stream as people hurried home after their day's work. Derrick could hear the regular clip of women heels on the sidewalk. He recognised Samantha instantly and stepped out from behind her and pulled her into the alley. Derrick muffled Samantha's scream with his hand as he propelled them both back further into the ally. Confident he would not be observed he pushed Samantha up against the wall.

Fear and recognition washed over Sam's face as she finally got a look at her attacker. Derrick's face came closer to hers, and she could smell the stench of stale tobacco smoke and heavy liquor. Derrick smiled with an evil look of one who has caught his prey, revealing a mouth full of yellowing teeth that completed the horrible vision before her. "So Miss Scott," Derricks words came out slightly slurred, "Been talking to the Farley's have we?"

Samantha's heart was pounding, How do I get out of this and warn Paula? She thought to herself. At this point, her natural instincts kicked in. Samantha steeled herself for her one shot, and she was pretty sure it would be her one and only chance. Suddenly Sam brought her right leg up and kneed Derrick in the groin. Her aim was spot on and had Derrick not have been half drunk he may have reacted just fast enough to avoid it, but the drink had dulled his reflexes, and Sam's knee made full contact with surprising power. Derrick crumpled to the ground as Sam pushed him further away and started to run for the street. If I can just get to the street, I will be safe. She told herself. Just as she reached the street, Samantha tripped, and her momentum continued to carry her forward. There was a sudden screech of breaks and a sickening thud as she was collected by a car.

Derrick saw it all unfold lying curled up in a foetal ball clutching his crutch. As Samantha ran off he knew he was doomed, suddenly she tripped and fell into the path of an oncoming car and Derrick watched as her body was catapulted through the air past the alleyway entrance and out of view. Derrick struggled to his feet and tried to walk as normally as possible. I have to check she's dead; he thought to himself as he battled rising nausea in his stomach. The scene on the road was chaos, people had jumped out of their cars hoping to help, but as Derrick saw, help would not be of any use for Samantha Scott.

Sam lay on the street; her right arm was folded under her body at an unnatural angle, and her clothes were ripped and torn from the impact with the road. But these paled in comparison to her head. Half of Sam's head was smashed in like a crumpled beer can and the pool of blood told Derrick all he needed to know. The sight was enough to release the building vomit as he crouched in the gutter purging some of the earlier drink. If people noticed, they assumed that it was the sight of the carnage that had set him off, not a kick to his nuts. As the sounds of sirens broke through the noise of the crowd, Derrick gathered himself up and wiped some vomit from his face. He needed to be as far away from here as soon as possible. This was not difficult as the attention was on the body on the street, not some guy walking away looking sick.

61

Dennis pulled up outside Sam's flat; he had decided that Paula's email might have spooked her so he had grabbed a bunch of flowers and popped over to say hi, and to reassure her everything would be ok. There was another car parked outside, a plain brown sedan. Dennis walked up to the door and knocked. The door opened to a man standing inside wearing a coat. "Can I help you sir?" he asked. Dennis was surprised, "Um, yes I am here to see Samantha, is she in?" he asked.

"Let him in Jeff." Another male voice said from inside. The guy who greeted him opened the door wider, and Dennis walked in unsure what was going on. A second man who, Dennis assumed was the owner of the voice he had heard, came over and introduced himself. "Hi, I'm Detective Chris Talbert, and this is Officer Jeff Simmons," Talbert said showing Dennis his badge. "You're looking for Miss Scott?" he asked.

"Yes what's happening, why are you here, where's Sam?" The questions tumbled out of Dennis.

"Sir perhaps you should sit down," Simmons replied. Dennis looked at the two police officers, "I would prefer to stand it that's ok, what is going on?" Dennis repeated.

Talbert knew from experience that there was no easy way to say it, "Miss Scott is dead. She was killed yesterday when she ran out in front of a car on Main Street," he replied.

Dennis turned white and slumped into a seat.

"Sir, do you mind telling us who you are and how you know Miss Scott?"

Dennis took a moment to gather his thoughts. "I'm Dennis Farley," Dennis said taking out his wallet and showing Jeff his drivers licence. "My wife and Sam, I mean Samantha are friends. Paula, my wife, is out of town and asked me to drop in on her and see if she was alright," Dennis replied looking at his shoes.

"And the flowers Mr Farley, do you regularly bring Miss Scott flowers when your wife is away?" Talbert's implied accusation hung in the air. "The flowers were for Sam; she had been feeling off-colour, and my wife had not heard from her in a few days. She asked me to bring these over and check on Sam," replied Dennis.

Talbert and Simmons exchanged a look that had 'bullshit' all over it. "Mr Farley, could you tell me what you were doing at 5 pm yesterday?" Talbert asked.

"Sure, I was running a lecture for thirty students at Ede University. Any one of my students there can vouch for me," Dennis snapped. Talbert nodded to Jeff who, taking out a notebook, jotted down the details of Dennis statement.

"What is happening here, Detective? I thought Sam was hit by a car?" Dennis asked, getting his head back in the game.

"We have witnesses that say they saw Miss Scott running away from an alleyway before her being hit by the car; they believe that she may have been chased or running away from someone. We are just covering every angle, Mr

Farley. We may need you to come into the station in the next few days so we can take more of a statement. I trust that will not be a problem?" Talbert asked.

"No, no problem just call me on any of my numbers," Dennis replied, handing Talbert a business card.

Jeff looked at Dennis Farley; he knew he was hiding something but he was unsure what it was. "Do you know if Miss Scott has any living relatives, Mr Farley?" he asked.

"Not that I am aware of, she said her mother and father had died quite young, and she was raised by her grandfather," he replied.

"And how long have you known Miss Scott?" he continued.

"My wife and Sam met over sixteen years ago, but I have only recently met her," Dennis truthfully replied.

"Ok, then Mr Farley, I don't think we have any further questions at this time, but we will call if we need any further information. Thank you for assisting us." Dennis left the flat and hopped back in his car, clearly in shock. It took him a few moments to find the keys and get it started; then he drove away slowly.

As Dennis drove off, Jeff noted down his plates. "You believe any of that?" he asked Talbert.

"Not a word, that guy is hiding something," Talbert replied.

"So why are we not taking him in and sweating him out?" Jeff asked.

"Because we have a maybe accident. I don't think this guy did it, but he is hiding something. I think he and Miss Scott have a thing going on that the wife doesn't know about, and the last time I checked, that wasn't illegal," Talbert replied. "Ok, let's finish up here. We got the mobile phone from the morgue, let's see if she has a laptop. Might even find some juicy emails from the two lovers," Talbert instructed. Jeff found the laptop five minutes later. "Hey Chris, I got the laptop, you want me to check the email?" he asked as Chris walked into the room.

"No, just bag it, forensics will have a look at it. They will have kittens if they find we have had a go at it first," he replied. "Ok, nothing else here of interest, nothing out of place, let's get back to the station and write this up."

62

Derrick had managed to change his flights last minute and on boarding he was happy to still have some alcohol in his system for the flight back as it helped dull his fears. The flight was mercifully smooth with very little turbulence, a fact that suited his bruised crotch very well. It was not the only part of him that was hurt; his ego had taken a pounding. How could you let a little bitch like that get the better of you, Pullman? He asked himself. On landing, Derrick collected his car from the long term parking and headed straight back to the office. The alcohol had deadened the pain, and his anger had mostly gone. Now he needed to plan his next move.

Dennis pressed the button on the garage door remote, and once it opened, he drove in. He waited while the door closed behind him. His hands were still shaking after learning of Samantha's death. He needed to call Paula and quickly. The one thing that was clear in his mind was that Sam had not died in an accident. Something or someone had got to her, and that meant that Daniel and the girls were also at risk. Dennis picked up the phone and called Paula's number. Paula picked up after the third ring. "Paula, it's Dennis, Sam is dead," Dennis blurted out.

"What the hell? What do you mean she's dead? What happened?" Paula replied. Dennis took a moment to describe what had happened at Sam's flat. Paula took it in quickly and came to the same conclusion as him.

"We have to get him out and now!" She stated. "It has to be today!" "I agree, how quickly can you get him?" Dennis asked. "Today, after school. I think it would be better to get him from Ash's or from School. That way we might still have an option of not spooking Kirkland," Paula explained.

"Do what you have to do, has Ben managed to submit the evidence to his Captain?" Dennis asked.

"I don't know, but I will ask, I am calling him now. Love you, wish us luck," Paula hung up the phone. Paula ran over to the motel office she was going to need to find the number of the police station. "Hi Paula, don't you look lovely today, just lovely," Lexi said in the way of a greeting. "What can I do for you today?"

"Hi Lexi, I need to borrow a phone book please," Paula replied. "Oh sugar, no problem, who ya trying to find?" Lexi asked not yet making a move to get the phonebook. Paula made a snap decision, "Lexi I need to call the police and speak to Ben Smith. James Kirkland is my biological son, and Ben is trying to build a case to arrest Dr Kirkland. Lexi, it is imperative that I get through to him quickly as my son may be at risk," Paula's statement had left Lexi speechless, a stunned expression was fixed on her face, at any other time, Paula would have laughed at the fact that Lexi didn't have anything to say.

Reaching below the counter Lexi produced the phonebook and calmly passed it over. Paula took the book, and as she was leaving the office, Lexi called out, "He sure looks a lot like the twins," she said.

"He's a triplet Lexi, he was born with Gina and Steph," Paula called out over her shoulder, as she ran back to her room, wishing she could see the look on Lexi's face right now.

Paula quickly found the correct number and called the police station. "Officer Ben Smith please, this is urgent," She said to the operator. The line rang four times.

"Ben Smith," came the answer.

"Ben it's Paula Farley. Daniel is at risk; we think Kirkland knows," Paula explained all that Dennis had said. Ben listened to Paula and took notes.

"Damn, a witness dead," Ben replied, after hearing about the death of Samantha. "Paula, I am due to see the Captain in about thirty minutes. I will contact Denver PD and get what they have and add it to my stuff. When do you want us to move on Kirkland?" He asked. Paula was flabbergasted, "Kirkland? I don't care one bit about, that piece of shit, Kirkland. Ben, get Daniel out and safe, then go after Kirkland!" Paula shouted down the phone.

"Ok, ok, got it loud and clear. You do know that if we do this wrong Kirkland could do a runner and we may never get him then?" Ben explained.

"I know Ben, but we all agreed that we would only keep him there as long as he was safe. That has changed with Sam getting killed," Paula reminded him.

"Ok, what number do I call you back on?" Paula gave Ben the number and hung up.

63

Ben clicked into his computer terminal and looked up the number for Denver Central Police. It rung a few times then was answered by a friendly voice. "Denver Central Police Department, how can we help you."

"Hi this is Officer Ben Smith of the Greenspan Police Department, I believe you have a case involving a woman by the name of Samantha Scott. I was wondering if I could speak to the lead detective?" Ben replied.

"One moment please," came the reply. There was a small delay as Ben's call was transferred.

"Chris Talbert, what can I do for you, officer?" Talbert asked, on picking up the line.

"Detective, I am working a case in Greenspan Texas, and one of the material witnesses was named Samantha Scott, of Denver. I have been led to believe that Miss Scott was reported dead yesterday," Ben advised.

Chris cursed under his breath. "Sorry who are you, and just how did you find this information?" Chris replied tersely.

"Detective Talbert, I am Detective Ben Smith, badge number 275643, of the Greenspan Police Department. I have been advised by Paula Farley, who is known to Miss Samantha Scott, that she is dead and that it is a possible homicide. Is this true?" Ben snapped back. Paula's surname snapped Talbert out of his annoyance, Farley, that was the name of the guy who visited Miss Scott's house, he thought to himself. "One moment please," came Talbert's reply as he checked Ben's badge and details.

Chris looked at his screen showing Ben's details as he came back to Ben, "I'm sorry Detective, I needed to check out your details. We often get the press trying to get information about cases by pretending to be police. Yes, we have an investigation into the death of Miss Scott and at present we can not rule out homicide," Talbert explained what the witnesses thought they had seen.

"So it could be an accident?" Ben asked hopefully.

"It could be but, it feels funny to me. I've got that feeling…" Talbert didn't finish; he knew that if Ben Smith were a decent cop he would know what he meant.

"Damn," Ben replied hoping for a different answer. "This is going to make things real ugly. Thanks for the info," he added.

Chris cut in before Ben could hang up, "Detective, can you tell me what the hell is going on, what have the Farley's got to do with this?" he asked, wanting to know how this all tied together.

Ben considered the request, then decided that sharing the info could be helpful, "I better be quick, I have to take this to my Captain in a few minutes. The Farley's are the parents of a boy who was abducted sixteen years ago by the doctor in charge of the birth. The nurse in attendance was Miss Scott. She became a Christian, finally felt guilty and told the Farley's. They are trying to get the kid back and put the doc away for good," Ben explained.

Talbert was shocked, "Holly crap, I thought that shit only happens in the movies. Can you send me your file as I need to build our case up as a homicide?" Talbert asked, "And, Ben, I'm sorry I was so abrupt with you before," he added.

"No problem, I am just going to see about a warrant and some protection for the family as this just got real. Thanks for the info, I will be in touch." Ben hung up.

The meeting with Captain Paulson went well. Ben presented all the evidence that the girls had collected, material from the safe and fake passports that Daniel had found and the affidavit from Samantha. The only thing he left out was the news of Sam's death. Paulson listened quietly nodding at various points in Ben's presentation. Ben had purposely presented all the facts and did not even leave out parts where he had delayed advising the Captain to give the Farley's more time to gather evidence. Ben knew he could be in line for a dressing down if this went badly but Daniel's safety was of higher importance.

Captain Paulson sat behind his desk and considered Ben, "This was quite a gamble, Ben," he pointed out.

"Yes sir it was, but the kids came through. I felt that without those documents the case would be shaky at best…" Ben explained as Paulson stopped him mid-sentence with a wave of his hand.

"Don't get me wrong Ben, what you did was a hell of a thing, real thinking on your feet. I'm glad it worked. So what do you now need from me?" Paulson asked. Ben sighed a sigh of relief. "Well, sir I need a search warrant for Kirkland's home, and office preferably conducted at the same time. To action those searches I will need two teams of six officers and probably some support from the traffic team to block a couple of roads. I also need a witness protection location that we can move the Farley family to as soon as possible." Ben replied. Paulson looked surprised, "Witness Protection? Where is the risk to the Farley's?" he asked.

Ben took a big breath, "That's the one bit I left out sir. Samantha Scott, the nurse that helped steal Daniel, was most likely murdered yesterday in Denver," Ben let this revelation hang for a moment. Before he could continue Paulson pressed the buzzer on his desk. "Julie I want a line to Judge Roscoe pronto, and get Craig Hammond from SWAT up here now," he barked down the line. Paulson stood up and moving to a combination safe in the corner removed an envelope and handed it to Ben. "Address and keys for the safe house. From now on only you and I know where they are. I think it is time to get the Farley's into safety don't you think Mr Smith?" Paulson asked. "Oh and Ben, don't try that leaving out stuff to the last minute thing ever again, or you might just find yourself on traffic duty for the rest of your natural life," Paulson added with a grin.

64

Ben called Paula's number, and she answered in two rings. "Be ready in ten minutes, I'm picking you up." He hung up not giving her time to ask questions. His next call was back to Chris Talbert. "Talbert I need a favour, I need you to pick up Dennis Farley and take him into protective custody. The witness protection program will pick up the tab," Ben added.

Chris grabbed a pen and some paper, "Sure thing, what do you want to us to do with him when we get him?" Talbert asked.

Ben stopped to think, "Not sure, put him up in a hotel with a guard until we can move him to the safe house here in Texas. That should do," Ben replied.

"No prob, I will get right on it. This is moving pretty fast now huh?" Talbert asked.

"Yup it is, I better go and hey Chris, thanks. Call me on this number when you have him," Ben gave Talbert his mobile number and hung up.

Jumping in his car, Ben raced over to Paula's motel. She was waiting outside and got in. "We're off to school," Ben said not waiting for the question. Ben and Paula pulled into the school parking lot and Ben parked in the disabled parking spot closest to the entrance. Getting out of the car, Ben was going to tell Paula to stay here but looking at her face he knew that would be a waste of breath. "Come on then, let's get this over with," he said heading towards the office. Paula noticed Ben had his sidearm strapped to his leg and that he was wearing a bulletproof vest of some kind. Ben approached the receptionist and flashed his badge as he walked past "Here to see Ms Jones," He stated, continuing to walk past.

The receptionist stood up as if to oppose the interruption, "Ms Jones doesn't like..." the rest of the receptionist's sentence trailed off as she realised Ben was not going to stop. Paula followed in Ben's wake into Mss Jones office.

"Um, hello," Jones said looking up from her computer, "I don't believe I have any appointments today," She replied briskly.

Ben handed her a piece of paper. "Ms Jones this is a warrant for me to take into protective custody the following pupils; Gina Farley, Stephanie Farley and Daniel Farley also known as James Kirkland," Ben let the news sink in.

Ms Jones had not yet caught up with what was going on, "But Mr?" Jones began not remembering Ben's name.

Ben helped her out, "That is Detective Ben Smith, Ms Jones," he advised, with emphasis on the word detective.

"Oh yes, of course, Detective Smith, I am sure you will understand that I cannot let the children go without express permission from their parents. Miss Farley here can account for Gina and Stephanie, but I will need to contact James's father to receive permission for him," Principal Jones replied desperately trying to gain control of the situation.

Ben leaned over the desk and pointing at the warrant, stared at Ms Jones, "Principal Jones, you will not under any circumstances speak to, or make contact with anyone regarding these children or you will be in contempt of this court issued warrant. If you do so, I will personally see to it that you are removed from your position here at the school and face the judge who issued this warrant to explain to him why he should not find you in contempt. Do I make myself clear?" Ben said, his voice raised. "You will now take Mrs Farley and me to collect Gina, Steph and Daniel right this minute." Principal Jones did not use to being ordered around, but the piece of paper in front of her made it quite clear she needed to do what Detective Smith said.

"Very well then," She said stiffly getting up from her desk, "This way." As she passed the receptionist, Ms Jones stopped, "What classes are the Farley children and James Kirkland in at present?" She asked.

The receptionist consulted her computer terminal. "4J, Ms Jones, Science, they are all in the same class," replied the receptionist. Her eyes were popping out of her head, as she had heard every word said in the principal's office.

Mrs Jones led the way to 4J and without knocking walked in. Ignoring the teacher she called Gina, Steph and James to come out. There was a murmur from the other students as this event was most definitely out of the ordinary. Gina, Steph and Daniel, got up, left their seats, as Daniel passed Ash she grabbed his hand, gave it a squeeze and smiled. Ben gave Ash a thumbs up as he turned and let the room. The three kids all gathered out in the hallway with Ben and Paula.

"Is it time?" Daniel asked.

Paula nodded and with tears in her eyes gave him the biggest hug. "Yes, son it's time to come home."

The Farley's had turned to leave when Principal Jones spoke up, "Detective, what do I say when Dr Kirkland calls asking where his son is?" Daniel turned back to her and glared, "Ms Jones, Dr Kirkland doesn't have a son," he replied, walking away with his family. They headed out to the waiting police car, leaving a ‘the Jones' very confused standing in the hallway.

65

In Denver, Chris Talbert was making an equally significant scene to the one Ben had made in Greenspan. One officer had already informed the Dean of the university they had to take Dennis, while Chris handled the man himself. Dennis was mid-lecture when Chris opened the door and came in. Daniel looked up from his notes expecting the interruption to have come from a late student trying to sneak in, but he recognised Chris straight away.

A knot of fear hardened in his stomach as Detective Talbert approached him on stage. "Mr Farley, we need to leave right now, no questions, you just have to come with me," Talbert announced loud enough for the students to hear. There was a murmur here, like at Greenspan. Dennis, not knowing what to do, gathered up his notes and dismissed his students.

"What's going on? Am I under arrest?" He asked. Talbert was tempted to say yes as he was still annoyed Farley had been less than honest about his visit to Samantha Scott, but his professionalism won through.

"You are under protective custody, Mr Farley. We have reason to believe that Samantha Scott was murdered and you and your family may be at risk," Talbert replied.

"Oh," Was all Dennis could manage, as he followed Talbert to the door. Talbert opened the it and a uniformed officer joined them as they walked out to a waiting police car. Talbert sat in the back with Dennis.

"My wife and kids, are they safe?" Dennis left the question in the air.

"I suspect they are being picked up like you, right now. We are going to take you to a hotel and keep you safe while the Texas P.D. work out a plan to get you and your family together. You know, this would have been much easier if you had been honest with me to start with Mr Farley," Talbert advised. Dennis just nodded.

Talbert dialled Ben on his mobile. "Ben, it's Chris, we have Mr Farley, and we are on route to a hotel. How is it going at your end?" Chris asked.

Ben's frustrated voice came over the line, "A bit slow going, the mother and I got the kid, and his sisters but the warrant for search of the Doc's place and office has been delayed. Damn public servants," Ben ranted down the line. "We're on our way to the safe house now. I will give you a call when we organise to get Dennis up here. I suspect it will be a public flight and that we will need an officer to assist with the delivery," Ben advised.

"Great, just let me know what we can do, hey I might even bring the package down myself," Chris replied grinning.

"That would be great; I will owe you a beer for all this. Thanks again Chris, will be in touch," Ben ended the connection.

Talbert turned to Dennis, "Your family are safe, including your son." Dennis looked relieved and had finally started to relax.

66

Simon Kirkland was tired; this was the third surgical operation today, and that was on top of his normal clinic load. Thankfully this patient was playing ball, and the c-section had gone well. Kirkland's Blackberry started to ring. "Nurse, get that please," Kirkland said as more of an order than request.

"Hello, Dr Kirkland's phone, Dr Kirkland is busy in an operation right now could he please call you back?" she asked. The nurse listened to the response, "ok just one moment please," she replied. "Sorry Dr Kirkland, it is your son's school principal and she says it is very urgent," The nurse advised.

"Nurse holds the phone up," Kirkland ordered. The nurse held the phone to Kirkland's ear.

"Kirkland here, what's the problem?" He barked down the line.

"I am so sorry to bother you, Dr Kirkland," came the voice of Principal Jones, "A police officer has just been to school and taken James away with him," The words came tumbling out of Principal Jones. "I tried to stop them but he took them, all three of them and they went off with Mrs Farley."

Simon's mind was racing. "Get a hold of yourself Ms Jones. Who did James go off with?" He demanded.

"I'm sorry, they told me not to contact you; it was Detective Smith, Paula Farley and her two girls Gina and Stephanie. The Detective said something about James's name not being James but Daniel. It was all so crazy, and it happened so quickly," She stammered.

Kirkland had gone deathly white, "Nurse, hang up please," he asked. "Tim, close up here, please. I, um, have a family emergency I need to deal with," Kirkland said, leaving the operating theatre. They know! He told himself as he got out of his scrubs. Oh God they know and now the police are involved. He slumped down onto the bench in the changing room. I have to get out while I can.

This was the first clear thought that came to his mind. Kirkland changed quickly into his day clothes and headed out to the carpark. I have prepared for this. I have an exit plan if that ungrateful son has thrown his lot in with the Farley's then so be it. He can stay behind. He thought to himself. His false sense of his importance and cunning was kicking in. No problem, this was always a possibility, I have planned for this.

The drive from the hospital to home was about thirty-five minutes. In that time Kirkland had convinced himself that everything was in control, or to his way of thinking, everything was in his control. Instead of pulling into his drive Kirkland drove around the block twice looking for any sign of the police. Everything looked normal; there were no cars out of place, so he decided to pull into his drive. Jumping out of the car he strolled up to his door as casually as possible just in case someone was looking. Entering his home he went straight to his study to retrieve the money and passports from the safe.

Ben watched Kirkland circle the block twice before stopping outside his house. He had only just managed to get inside his home about three minutes before Kirkland drove past. Speaking into his two-way radio he signalled the others, "Suspect is entering his house, close off the street but stay out of sight. No lights, and no sirens." he ordered.

Two squad cars at each end of the street moved into position blocking the two possible escape routes.

67

For Ben, it had been a race against time. Firstly he had to get the Farley's to the safe house. They were there now guarded by two plain clothed officers both with MP5 machine guns. Ben was fairly sure that their location was unknown to the Kirkland's but the two armed officers were his insurance policy. It was pretty clear that Kirkland had a lot to lose.

The information the kids had unearthed detailed over twenty-five years of abducted babies and they represented an enormous sum of money; it was dynamite. Some of the 'clients' who purchased these children were influential people who might also be a threat to the Farley's safety. Ben was not taking any chances with Dr Kirkland. He and four other officers quickly dressed in black tactical gear. Each of the four officers attached an H & K MP7 submachine gun to fast action slings and checked their personal side arms. Ben preferred not to carry the bulk of the MP7 and instead carried two P30 pistols, one holstered to each leg. Each officer checked each other over to ensure they were ready. Ben checked both his guns to ensure the safeties were on and that they had a full clip and one round loaded ready in the barrel. "Ready guys?" he asked.

"Ready," Came the reply in unison. Ben explained the plan assigning two of the team to cover the back door of the house. He and the remaining members of the team would enter the house.

"Remember, we don't want this to end in bloodshed, so only fire if you believe you, or someone else, is at risk."

The team moved out down to the Kirkland's. They moved swiftly from one area of cover to then next. The hardest part was the last thirty feet. It was across the Kirkland's lawn, and there was no cover. They dashed the last few feet and formed up together against the wall of Kirkland's house. Ben indicated for the back door team to move, he glanced at his watch; they would need about a minute to get into place.

Kirkland went down to his study and removed the family painting from the wall. He looked at the painting as he took it down and felt no connection to the boy in the picture. To Kirkland, James was dead. Spinning the combination from memory he opened the safe and removed the notebooks, cd, disks and USB memory stick. Opening the notebooks flat he fed them through his shredder.

The machine made a protesting sound as it chewed through each book. Kirkland picked up the cd-rom and disks and feed them in as well. The machine made a mechanical screaming sound as the cd and discs burst into hundreds of fragments. Kirkland was pretty sure the shredder was stuffed, but it had served its purpose. Taking the shredded contents over to his open fire he poured it on and set it alight. Kirkland watched as the paper pieces burned and the plastic remnants began to melt.

The USB stick he dropped into in his pocket, it was encrypted, so he was pretty sure it was safe from prying eyes. Reaching into the safe Kirkland withdrew the envelope with the passports and the thousands of dollars. He poured the contents onto his desk. Kirkland suddenly went cold. Instead of what should have been there, the $150,000 and the passports, all that fell out was a single book. Simon picked it up and examined the spine. 'The HMS Revenge', one of his books from his library. Simon collapsed into his chair.

Ben and his team had found the front door unlocked and had quietly entered the house. They were now searching room by room having let the back door team in quietly. Ben clearly heard Simon Kirkland in his study, Ben grinned to himself and indicated to the two officers what he was going to do.

Ben stepped into the room and yelled, "Freeze, Police, put your hands up right now." It always sounded silly, but it had to be said. Simon just stood there as the three police officers pointed their weapons at him The look on Simon's face said it all. He knew he was caught, but he was confident he would remain free as he had destroyed the evidence. Simon raised his hands with a slight smile on his face. Ben moved in and cuffed Simon's hands behind his back while the two other officers kept their guns pointed at both of the Kirkland's. Once secured Ben spoke into his radio, "Lead to all units, suspect in custody, no shots fired. Roadblock cars close into suspects house and maintain perimeter."

Ben sat Simon down and read him his rights. "I have nothing to say, without my lawyer present," Simon replied dejectedly.

Ben looked over at the dying fire, "Just to let you know, Dr Kirkland, we already have copies of all the notebooks, the CD Rom and the USB memory stick. Add to that the murder of Nurse Samantha Scott, and you will be spending a very long time behind bars." Ben looked at Kirkland, who had gone very white.

"Nurse Scott was murdered?" He asked. Ben nodded, thinking to himself that perhaps Kirkland had not been involved in Samantha's murder, "Oh don't worry Dr Kirkland we will have a real big chat to you back at the station," Ben replied. Ben looked over at one of the uniformed officers who had just arrived, "Oh good, your ride is here. Pete, please escort Dr Kirkland to the squad car, he has an appointment back at the station," Ben smiled he knew this case was as tight as possible.

Ben was going to see if anyone would take a wager on Dr Kirkland's lawyer trying to bargain a better deal by midday tomorrow. He doubted anyone would bet against him on this one. Pulling out his mobile, he dialled Paula. "Ben?" Came the questioning response from the line.

"We got him, Paula, the kids, were right, he was going to make a run for it. I am not sure where he was going to go, but we will get to the bottom of it soon," Ben replied to the unasked question.

"What about Dennis?" Paula asked.

"We had some friends at the Denver P.D. pick him up and keep him safe at a hotel," Ben paused, not sure if he should tell her the next part, "Paula, my gut tells me Kirkland didn't personally kill Samantha Scott. I think he has someone working for him. Till I can confirm it, either way, I would prefer you guys to stay put. I will have an officer pick up some personal effects from the motel and take them back to the station, and I will bring them to you tonight when this has all calmed down a bit," he advised.

Paula thanked Ben and hung up; the twins had sat one each side of Daniel the whole way through the call.

Daniel, looked up at Paula, "It's over isn't it?" he asked. Paula just nodded. The three kids hugged one another tight. Paula could see it was a moment she should not intrude on. There on the sofa were her three babies all grown up but still needing each other, connected in an amazing way. Paula saw this was an incredibly emotional moment for Daniel, but the girls 'felt' his need rather than saw it. Paula left the room to call Dennis and give him the news. The kids needed space right now and although Paula felt somewhat excluded she understood. Calling Dennis helped to settle her emotions; he had always been the safe harbour for her in times of storms.

68

Ben and his team walked back to his house. All their gear lay scattered around Ben's lounge. Ben opened the door and sitting on the sofa surrounded by their gear was Ash. "You boys are slobs," She announced, "Did my Dad get shot, cause he's not really that fast," she added. The team laughed, most of them had known Ash since she was a toddler, so her digs at her father were nothing new. Ben crashed down on the sofa next to Ash. "Hey, so how was school?" he asked.

"Well, you know that guy I have been dating? Well, some stupid arse cop and his real mother come barging in and drag his sexy bod and his twin sisters out of my class," she replied grinning.

"You see that was the problem, you think he has a sexy bod," Ben replied, joking. That earned him a punch in the upper arm.

"Where's my boyfriend dad? You just can't make people disappear when they date your daughter," Ash insisted.

"Um, yes I can, I'm a policeman, I know the very best places to bury a body," Ben replied, loving this exchange with his daughter. "DAD!" Ash replied rapidly getting annoyed.

"Oh, alright, Your beloved, and his family are in witness protection, and they are quite safe. If, and only if, you are nice to me, I might take you over to see them later. Perhaps you could get us men, all a can of soda, which might help me make up my mind," Ben grinned.

"Fine, I will get your soda's, but you and your men can get your dirty guns off the sofa's," Ash said, having the last word as she headed for the kitchen.

Derrick sat in his office re-reading the email he had forwarded from Samantha's computer. He needed to clean up this mess and was trying to figure out who needed to be taken care of first. The email seemed to say that this Ash-kid has a copy of the information. She would be the best person to start with. Derrick double clicked on Internet Explorer and typed in an image search for Ash and Greenspan. The results appeared on his screen moments later. Several were pictures of a teenage girl with short cropped hair holding various trophies. Derrick clicked on one of the most recent.

> "Greenspan Press
>
> Local girl wins shooting competition.
>
> Ashlie Smith, daughter of local Detective Ben Smith, takes out the woman's division of the Steel Target Shooting Competition. Miss Smith, who prefers to be known as Ash, dominated the competition posting scores that were competitive with the men's divisions. 'Ash had taken an interest in shooting since the death of her mother at an early age. We both enjoy it; it's a way for us to stay connected.' Ben Smith said."

Derrick had his girl. A quick look up in the telephone book confirmed his suspicions. B. Smith, listed on the same street as the Kirkland house, just a few doors down. No doubt Ash and the Kirkland kid were childhood sweethearts. Oh, wouldn't it be good if he forced the Kirkland kid to watch him extract some information from little Miss Smith? Derrick quickly gave up the idea, although it would be fun, it would complicate the job significantly. No, just him and Ash would be okay. He would need to watch the house and find a time she was alone. Perhaps when Daddy dearest went to work. Daddy could be a problem, but cops were all stupid as far as Derrick was concerned. After all, they did pretty much what he did, but he got paid much more to do it. Derrick hopped in his car and headed over to the Smiths.

Ben and the team had changed back into their regular clothes. The four officers who were part of the raid had walked back over to the Kirkland's place to assist with searching the house for any more evidence. Ben loaded his tactical gear back into the trunk of his car and headed over to help out. The team were just finishing up as he arrived. "Find anything?" he asked.

"Not really, we have bagged a USB memory stick, that was on Dr Kirkland's person and removed a couple of computers for Forensics to go over, but the rest of the house is clean," the officer in charge of the scene replied.

"What about his office?" Ben asked.

"Same story over there, couple of computers seized and not much else."

Ben nodded, "Ok leave a guy inside, relieve him every four hours but use a plain car, no back 'n' whites. We might get lucky if someone calls in."

Ben walked back to his house to tell Ash where he was going. "Ash, I'm going to get some paperwork done then I will be back to take you over to see Daniel and the Farley's," Ben called out.

"Ok, see you later," Ash replied from upstairs. Derrick had only just pulled up a few doors down from the Smiths house when he saw a man in uniform come out the front door and drive off. Well, that made life easier. He thought to himself. No time like the present. Derrick got out of his car and headed up to the Smiths front door.

69

Chris Talbert sat at his desk reviewing the Scott case and the material from Greenspan that Ben had sent over. The phone on his desk started to ring. "Talbert," he answered.

"Hi Chris, this is Tom from Forensics, we have found something on the Scott laptop. Miss Scott received an email from a Paula Farley about a Dr Kirkland."

Chris interrupted Tom, "Can you tell if she read it," he asked. "No, but we can say that someone read it and what is fascinating is someone forwarded it to another email address. I wouldn't have thought much about that if they had not tried to delete all sign of the forward," Tom replied.

"Who was it forwarded to Tom?" Chris asked. "It was forwarded to an email address of a two-bit private investigator based in Texas, Derrick Pullman. I'm sending you a copy of the email now for your case file," Tom explained.

"Hey thanks, Tom, good work." Chris had a bad feeling about this; it looked like someone had been side Samantha Scott's flat and forwarded this email on. Chris picked up the phone and dialled Ben.

"Ben Smith." Came the reply moments later.

"Ben, it's Chris in Denver. We have a lead on another suspect. It looks like a private investigator by the name of Derrick Pullman broke into Miss Scott's flat and forwarded an email from Paula Farley to his address. He tried to cover it up, but our IT nerds say he botched it," Chris explained.

"Great work Chris, do you happen to have a copy of the email?" Ben asked.

"Sure I will send it over, you want me to read you what it says?" Chris asked. "Yea, thanks," Ben replied listening to Chris read out the email. Ben thought it was pretty harmless until Chris got to the part about Ash and Daniel having evidence.

"Shit," He interrupted Chris, "that's my daughter."

Chris was shocked, "Christ Ben, your daughter, is mixed up in all of this? If that mutt went after Samantha Scott, he might just try for anyone else who knows," Chris was voicing the same concerns that were building in Ben.

"Chris I have to go." Ben hung up and quickly dialled home, there was no answer.

70

Derrick had quietly opened the Smiths front door and let himself in. "Who the hell are you?" Ash asked, standing in the middle of the lounge. "I work for Dr Kirkland," Derrick replied pulling out a Smith and Wesson 36 Special revolver. Derrick loved the look of fear on Ash's face.

The feeling of power over life and death was exhilarating. Derrick motioned over to the chair with the gun, indicating where he wanted Ash to sit. Ash moved slowly; her mind was racing, looking for any out she could find. She recognised the type of handgun but not the make or model. It would be about a 38 cal with five shots. Any one of which could end her life in a heartbeat. She told herself. Just thinking about the details was helping her to control her fear.

The phone rang, and nobody moved. Ash hoped it was her father and that her not picking up would provide him with a clue that she was in trouble. She needed to stall for time. "So what do you want?" She asked with more courage than she felt.

"I want to have a little talk. I want to know what information you took from Dr Kirkland?" Derrick replied, "And you are going to tell me everything I want to know or I am going to make you very uncomfortable," Derrick replied menacingly.

Ash decided that telling him everything was her best bet to stall for time. "We raided Dr Kirkland's safe, it took us ages to find the combination, but we finally realised it was the type of cigars he smokes," Ash continued. "We found notebooks full of information…" Ash was cut off by the sound of a knock at the door. Derrick moved behind the door as it opened and then smashed the door into the face of the uniformed officer trying to enter. The officer stumbled into the room partially stunned. Derrick took the opportunity to pistol whip the back of his head, and he went down like a tonne of bricks. Ash jumped up out of her seat screaming at Derrick to stop. She covered the downed officer's body with her own as a shield. Derrick had his pistol pointed directly at Ash.

Ash looked up at Derrick, "You shoot me and you will never know what we found," she spat out at him. The sound of a car pulling into the driveway had Derrick turning towards the sound. Still holding the gun at Ash, he pushed the door closed again. Derrick was going to use the same trick as before.

Ash waited, she knew it was her dad and she was about to walk into an ambush. She forced her breathing and heart rate down while sliding her right hand down to the officers holstered sidearm. Unclipping the holster she continued to look straight at the man with the gun. Her hand wrapped around the handle of the pistol and her thumb instinctively went to the safety lever.

It was a P30; she was sure, not the small version she usually used but most likely the L series her father liked. She clicked the safety off; the click sounded loud to her ears, but the guy with the gun didn't seem to hear. Ash saw the handle of the front door begin to move; it was now or never. Time rapidly slowed as Ash pivoted her whole body around to face the gunman. Ash could see her father pushing open the door as she brought up the pistol and sighted it on the gunman.

Derrick had readied himself to attack the next person coming through the door, and it was only at the last moment did he see Ash's movement through his peripheral vision. In a split second decision, he turned to face the movement. His brain had recognised the pistol scant moments before he felt the impact of the three rounds punching him in the chest.

Pumped up on adrenaline, Derrick stumbled backwards but felt no pain as Ben rushed into the room. Derrick was still holding his pistol as Ash fired another three rounds, this time into Derrick's right shoulder. The first round passed through the flesh but the second and third smashed into Derrick's shoulder blade sending him screaming to the ground as the gun dropped from his hand.

Ben had his sidearm out in a moment, but it was clear Ash had done what had needed to be done. The sounds of police sirens began to enter into Ash's consciousness. Ben knelt down beside her and making sure the safety was on, pried her fingers from the gun. "Are you ok?" He asked. Ash didn't reply; she buried her head against her father's chest her whole body shaking.

On the other side of the room, Derrick had stopped moving, a pool of blood was forming from under his body where two of Ash's rounds had smashed through an artery. Blood had bubbled up between Derrick's teeth making the already horrible yellow stains look even worse. Ben sat rocking his sobbing daughter as various officers rushed into the room soon to be followed by paramedics.

71

Six years later.

"You ready for this Ash?" Ben asked as Ash lay on the hospital bed her long black hair draped over the pillow, her face bathed in sweat.

"Well it's more than a little late to change my mind now isn't it," she quipped, as another contraction hit and she squeezed her father's hand. "Where the hell is Daniel? That boy moves fast enough on the track; you think he would get here fast for this," Ash announced, as Daniel entered the room with an orderly.

"It's time; they want to do a c-section. But don't worry I will be right there with you," Daniel said, gripping her hand. "Dad, tell Paula not to worry," Ash said as the orderly and Daniel guided the bed out of the room.

Paula sat in the waiting room with Dennis, the girls and Ben. "How do you think they are doing?" She asked Gina and Steph. "He's excited and nervous," Steph replied, referring to their strange connection to Daniel.

"I think he has been hiding something," Gina announced.

Paula suddenly looked concerned, "You think something is wrong with the baby?" she asked.

"No, I'm not sure, he just seems to have been super sneaky of late," Gina replied.

"Gets that from you, dear," Dennis announced, as he patted Paula's hand.

They all looked up as the door opened and the surgeon came through. "Congratulations, you can come and see them now, but we need to keep the visit short, Ashlie is exhausted, but she has come through like a trooper. They all got up and followed the surgeon through to Ashlie's room. Paula was the first into the room and looked at Ashlie lying in bed and Daniel standing next to her. Her son had a triumphant grin on his face, and Ashlie smiled a tired but happy smile. Swaddled in Ashlie's arms were not one, but two new-born babies.

"Twins! You had twins?" Paula cried out as he rushed to the bedside. Gina, Steph, Dennis and Ben came in behind her.

Paula spun around to Gina and Steph. "You two knew," she said, in the way of an accusation.

"Well we didn't know, but we had a bit of a niggle," Gina replied grinning.

Daniel moved to his mother's side, "Mum, meet your new grandchildren, Samantha and Samuel," Daniel grinned.

Paula, had tears streaming down her face, "You named them after Sam?"

The question didn't need answering, but Daniel did anyway, "It seemed like the right thing for us to do." he replied.

ABOUT THE AUTHOR

Nathan Monk has led a diverse life, having worked as retail clerk, information technology support engineer, sailing instructor, photographer, pastor and is currently working as a secondary teacher. He has had a few articles published in magazines. This is his first full-length novel. He lives in New Zealand with his wife and three children.

Made in the USA
Middletown, DE
07 January 2021